LINEAR TACTICAL SERIES

FOREVER

FOREVER: LINEAR TACTICAL

This book is dedicated to my cousin Hannah and her husband Tommy, two of my favorite people in the world.

And, like Ethan and Jess...knew they were meant to be together from the time they were kids.

CHAPTER ONE

SEVEN YEARS Ago
Ethan - 17
Jess - 14

ETHAN BOLLINGER HAD NEVER PLANNED to be hitchhiking out
of his hometown of Oak Creek, Wyoming.

Why would he need to? He had his own car, not to mention
he knew nearly every single person in the entire town, and
they knew him. He'd lived here his whole life.

But tonight, he needed to get to Reddington City without
anyone knowing about it. From there, he'd be taking a bus to
just outside Chicago.

This was his plan. He knew it was where he needed to go.
But every step he took away from Oak Creek was painful.

He was hitchhiking because he couldn't risk asking for a
ride. If he did, it would get back to Jess. And if she found out,
this was all over. He'd barely had the strength to walk away
from her today when she'd had no idea he wouldn't be coming
back.

There was no way he'd be able to do it if she asked him to stay.

He'd kissed her tonight knowing it was the last time he'd be kissing her for a long time, and the thought of it had gutted him. The thought of being without Jess had cracked something deep inside.

But how could he stay? For weeks now, he'd been listening to her talk about the Vandercroft Institute Fellowship, a unique research and educational grant based in London that was offered to very few. She'd be skipping high school altogether and combining her undergrad and graduate studies, plus participating in cutting-edge biotech research.

They'd sought Jess out. Maybe it was her perfect SAT scores in the fifth grade. Maybe it was the international science symposium where she'd caught the attention of everyone in her field. But the institute had figured out what Ethan had known since he'd met her when she was four years old.

Jess was a genius and was going to change the world.

Of course, there'd been no talk of sending her off to Vandercroft alone. Cade and Peyton, Jess's mother and father, weren't about to let their fourteen-year-old daughter move to a different continent by herself. Jess might be a genius, but she was still only fourteen.

Cade's profession as a country music superstar gave him a unique lifestyle. If he needed to take a few months off to hang out with his daughter in a different country, he could. And Peyton would just pack up Jess's little sister, Ella, and bring her along. That's what family did.

Jess had been talking about Vandercroft for weeks. They'd already flown her out to see the lab and the research she would be participating in. For the first time in her life, Jess would be working with people who were just as smart as she was and challenging her to do more.

Ethan knew enough about his little genius to know that

while that was scary for her, it was exactly what she needed and ultimately what she wanted. Vandercroft was where Jess needed to go.

But a few days ago, she'd started talking about *not* going, staying in Oak Creek, staying with *him*. They'd been lying out on the bales of hay, like always, to talk. She hadn't wanted to tell her mom and dad that she was thinking about turning the fellowship down, but she'd been willing to tell Ethan because they told each other everything.

And lying there on their favorite place, holding hands the way they always had, with her telling him that she wanted to be with him more than she ever wanted to do anything else, Ethan had known.

He had to leave.

Not because he didn't want to be with her, but because he *did*. Because he wanted to spend every moment of every day with her, but he also wanted her to be everything she could be. He loved her. He couldn't remember a time when he hadn't loved her.

He couldn't allow her to walk away from this opportunity. It was too big. Too important. But arguing with Jess was nearly impossible if she was set against it.

She was too smart. She could find every loophole or flaw in an argument. And although she'd never been cruel or vindictive, she could find every weakness someone had and use it against them.

And she knew his particular weakness. Her. The fact that he didn't want them to be separated by an ocean any more than she did.

Ethan had known he wouldn't be able to out-argue her on this. She would find a way to bring him around to her way of thinking, not that it would be hard.

So he'd done the only thing he could do. This morning, he'd entered his high school's office and withdrawn himself. He had enough credits to graduate, even without finishing this last quarter. It had meant forging his parents' signatures, since he was only seventeen, and praying Principal Renninger wouldn't call them to confirm.

He'd told the principal the truth: he was joining the military. That had seemed to satisfy the man. It was a logical conclusion for someone like Ethan. It had been what his dad had done. Hell, most of the Linear Tactical guys—Ethan's extended family—were former military.

He'd spent an afternoon writing letters to Jess and his parents, letters he could write because they'd worked tirelessly to help him overcome his dyslexia and reading difficulties. The letters weren't long, Ethan had never been long-winded, but he'd wanted them to know that he loved them. That he was making a choice that he would've made anyway, just a few months early.

And he'd especially wanted Jess to know that he was not saying goodbye. She was still the only one for him. But for right now, this was what needed to happen. She needed to go to London and step into her future. He would join the military like he'd planned.

By the time Jess got her letter and understood what he'd done, he'd be on the bus from Reddington City to Chicago. By the time she could do anything about it, he would already be enlisted and beyond her reach. She'd have no reason to sacrifice her future since he wasn't going to be around.

But even knowing in his heart of hearts that this was the right thing to do, that it was the decision that meant he and Jess would be together in the long run, each step was agony. Like he was being slowly torn in half .

That was pretty damned accurate.

A vehicle came up behind him, slowing down, and he stuck his thumb out in the air. It probably wasn't the safest thing to hitchhike anywhere, but he'd take his chances. When he turned to face the vehicle that had slowed down behind him, he let out a curse.

"Damn it." He should've recognized the sound of Dad's ancient Jeep ten miles back.

His dad had one arm slung over the steering wheel as he stopped next to Ethan and turned to look at him. "You need a ride?"

Ethan walked over and leaned on the Jeep door. "Depends. Are you going to take me back home?"

"Is home where you want to be?" Finn asked.

Yes. "I have to leave, Dad. I'm enlisting."

"I heard. I'll give you a ride to Reddington City."

He got in the Jeep. "How did you find out?"

Finn pulled back onto the road. "Principal Renninger. I ran into him at the gas station. Dude was chastising me for not encouraging you to finish high school. Said just because I ran off at seventeen to enlist didn't mean I should encourage you to do the same."

Ethan leaned his head back against the headrest. His dad had had this old Jeep his whole life. "I can't stay. If I stay, Jess will stay. She won't take that fellowship in London. College isn't for me, you know that. I knew I was going to enlist after graduation. This just upped the timetable a little."

Finn smiled over at him. "College was never for me either."

He'd known his dad would understand his desire to join the military. His dad wasn't going to be happy about Ethan's ultimate choice, but Finn Bollinger understood the desire to serve one's country.

"What does Jess think about this idea?" Finn asked.

Ethan rolled his eyes. "I'm here in one piece, aren't I? I may not be as smart as she is, but I'm smart enough to know that telling her about this plan ahead of time would have been a disaster."

"She's going to be pissed."

"I know, but ultimately it's the right thing to do. I love her enough to step out of her way. Not forever, but for right now."

"Well hell, son, it's hard to argue with that. Jess gets a lot of credit for how incredible she is. I don't think you get nearly as much as you deserve for how incredible *you* are."

"This isn't about being incredible. This is about loving her." It was that simple.

It was easy to put Jess's best interests at the forefront because he loved her. And also because he knew that her best interests were his best interests also.

Finn shook his head. "You're seventeen. You're making decisions like someone twice your age. Smart decisions, unselfish decisions. Jess may be the genius, but you're the greatest kid we've all ever known. When I think of you when I first got you, that little boy who wouldn't talk, the things that might've been done to you . . ."

Ethan reached over and touched his dad's arm. He knew Finn blamed himself for the things that had happened before he'd known about his son before he'd been able to get custody. Ethan's biological mother had been an addict before she'd died, and the abuse in his first three years had been significant.

But Finn had spent every single moment since the day he'd taken custody of Ethan showing him what true love meant and teaching him how to grow stronger than past demons.

"Everything I learned, I learned from you. You and Mom have been my example of how to be strong and how to love, and in Mom's case, how to fight dirty when needed." Charlie was his mother in every way but biological. "I'm okay. Look at me, Dad. I'm okay."

Finn glanced over and nodded, smiling. "You're a hell of a lot more than okay, and I'm glad Charlie taught you how to fight dirty. Speaking of"—he grabbed a set of folded papers that were sitting on the dash and handed them to Ethan—"your mom said not to start off your military career illegally. We signed your underage enlistment paper."

Ethan grinned. "Thank you. And thank you for understanding."

"So, you going to catch a bus in Reddington City? Where are you heading? Fort Benning, Fort Jackson?"

Ethan's eyebrow rose. "Did you not read the papers that you signed?"

"No, I just signed where Charlie told me to."

Ethan chuckled. This was going to be fun. He might be walking to Reddington City after all. "No, I'm headed for Recruit Training Command, Great Lakes."

Finn's head looked like it was going to spin all the way off. "RTC? You're joining the fucking *Navy*? I take back every good thing I've ever said about you. Fucking Navy. No wonder your mother told me to just shut up and sign. I never would have agreed to this ridiculous . . ."

Ethan smiled and looked out the window as his dad continued his diatribe for the next five miles.

But the important thing was, he kept driving. Finn Bollinger didn't like that his son was not joining the army and going into the Special Forces like he had, but he kept driving Ethan where he needed to go.

And when they arrived at the Reddington City bus depot, Finn shook Ethan's hand before pulling him in for a hug.

"Fucking Navy," he whispered in Ethan's ear. "My son is going to be a squid."

"It's what I want, Dad. My path isn't yours."

Finn hugged him tighter. "I've always known that. You be safe."

"I'm going to be more than safe, Dad. I'm going to be a Navy SEAL."

7

CHAPTER TWO

I sat down on a bench and took in a spoonful of my cherry Italian ice. The stuff had always been my favorite. Not quite a sorbet, not quite a snow cone . . . just cold deliciousness. Better than ice cream, although Jess would fight me on that one.

There'd been multiple times in my seven-year Navy career when I would've traded my next paycheck for the icy goodness, but there hadn't been any around. Usually because I was out to sea or in a country where there was hardly clean water, much less frozen desserts.

And hell, even when I hadn't been somewhere extreme, I hadn't been able to find my favorite treat. Stationed in Naples, I'd found out the hard way that Italy did not, in fact, sell Italian ice. They sold granitas, which were basically slushees, and gelato, which was ice cream. But no Italian ice.

So sitting here on a bench in Norfolk, Virginia, four days

past my last day on active-duty status, enjoying my Italian ice seemed like the right thing to do.

Much better than sitting in my one-bedroom apartment trying to figure out how to piece my life back together. Trying to figure out a strategy when it came to Jess.

I'd never thought I would need one. I'd been in love with Jess O'Conner forever, since we were both kids and hadn't even known what that meant. Naively, I'd thought our relationship would flow directly into marriage without a hiccup. That it was only a matter of time until we were both ready.

Until I'd shown up at her twenty-first birthday party two months ago and seen her practically draped over some other guy, using the flirtatious smile I'd only ever seen her use with me.

The memory still hit me in the chest. I'd never thought I was the jealous type, but I'd never had a reason to be jealous before. Jess and I were made for each other, and we'd always known that.

But it was silly of me to assume that people couldn't change. Especially someone with a brilliant brain like Jess's. My little genius was able to process information faster than anyone I'd ever known.

But I wasn't giving up, that was for damned sure. Maybe she needed to have a fling with this guy. I didn't like it, but I'd spent a lifetime learning strategy from the best. My dad and uncles at Linear Tactical came at everything—including their love lives—strategically. Seven years in the Navy had honed those strategic instincts in me.

It was time to come up with a new plan for dealing with Jess. But first, I was going to finish this Italian ice.

Or I thought I was.

Engines revved and then tires squealed behind me. I turned as three black SUVs pulled up to the curb in tandem. Men in suits emerged from each one, two of them staying put while one came toward me. I stood.

"Ethan Bollinger?"

I nodded, my body already at attention from years of habit. "Yes."

"We need you to come with us."

This wasn't the first time this had happened to me. As a SEAL, sometimes there wasn't time to do things the normal way, so I'd been picked up in the infamous black vehicles more than once. But I was out. My name shouldn't be on the docket for any missions or anything that would require me to leave without notice.

"I'm no longer on active duty," I said. "Are you sure you have the right person?"

"Yes," the man said without hesitation. "We'll drive your car back to your apartment complex while you're taken to the airport. Your keys, sir?"

I took them out of my pocket and handed them over as I stood and tossed the remaining Italian ice—*damn it*—into the nearby trash. I followed the man back to the SUVs, and they ushered me into one, closing the door behind me.

Just over an hour later, I was stepping off a Sea Hawk at Andrews Air Force Base near DC. The men with me in the helo hadn't been talkative, and I hadn't asked any questions. I knew better by now, and odds were they'd been tasked with getting me to where I was going and nothing more. They probably didn't know a thing.

This wouldn't have been anything out of the normal for me a week ago. But now it didn't make sense. It had to be some kind of paperwork mix-up. Since I was only a few days out of active duty, it was possible that they still had me on a go list somewhere.

I expected to be led into one of the small offices here on base to get a breakdown of what was happening, but there were yet more SUVs waiting for us at a safe distance. One of my companions held the door for me as I climbed inside.

In my years as a SEAL, I'd gotten used to the tense silences on drives like this. There wasn't any point in asking or speculating about what was happening. It was a waste of words. I'd find out soon enough.

So I did what I knew how to do best: listen, observe, analyze. Skills developed in me by my upbringing, then sharpened in my military career.

We drove for another half hour across the Virginia border and passed signs for Falls Church before we left the highway. I wasn't intimately familiar with the area, but I knew it was a wealthy suburb. A lot of high-end houses and rich families, including high-ranking military officials.

This was making less and less sense, but I couldn't say that I wasn't curious.

The driver stopped in front of a large, isolated house, and I was escorted inside by both the driver and the secondary. Not what I'd expected. But then, none of this had been what was expected.

Men waited for us inside. Three of them. But only one was familiar, and that was all I needed to realize this was more serious than I had thought.

General William Moss turned from the window as I entered, looking me up and down. He wasn't in uniform, but I didn't need that to recognize him. Any SEAL worth his salt would recognize the former commander of US Special Ops.

He'd been my boss a few years ago, in that same way you could say "the president is my boss" when you were in the military simply because he was the commander in chief. Too far up the chain for us to interact personally, but you knew who was signing your checks and giving the go orders on your missions.

The other two men were strangers but gave distinctly

different impressions. A tall man was pacing back and forth across the room when we entered. He was red, sweating, and visibly upset. The fact that we had arrived seemed to make him even more anxious. He ran a hand through his hair and glared at me before continuing to trace his chosen path across the floor.

In the opposite corner of the room from the general was a third man of Asian descent. Body language told me that he was also tense and upset but was handling it far better than the pacer. He watched me quietly, like he was assessing me for something, though I didn't know what.

The general nodded to my two companions, and they disappeared back outside, leaving me alone with the three men and thoroughly confused. This wasn't how I had imagined my day going, and there was a part of me that still thought this was a mistake.

General Moss turned to me. "Do you know who I am?"

I moved into a parade rest stance out of habit. "Yes, sir, General Moss. Though I'll admit that I don't know why I'm here."

His mouth turned into a deeper frown. "There's a potential international situation that we're trying to keep from getting out of hand."

"General," the quiet man said, "we agreed not to divulge details until everyone arrived."

"What does it matter, Yang?" the pacing man snapped. "If we're going to send a child into the situation, might as well tell him everything now to scare him off."

I noted the name he used and brushed off the insult about my age. That was nothing new for me. I'd gotten that my entire career. I was young for the things that were currently listed on my resume. But people got over my age quickly once they saw what I was capable of.

Glancing at the general, I raised an eyebrow and nodded to

the side of the room away from the two others. "May I speak to you, sir?"

He nodded once, joining me. "Yes?"

I kept my voice low and even. "General, I have to ask, are you sure that you have the right person? I'm no longer a SEAL. My release from active duty was this week. Don't get me wrong, I'm flattered and want to help, but an international incident sounds like you'll need a fully active team. I'm not that."

"I'm aware."

"And I'm a field medic, sir. Of course, I'm combat trained, but if you're looking for a one-man strike force, there are better options than me."

The man gave me a grim smile. "Don't worry, Bollinger, you're here for a reason. And a damn good one. You'll want to be here."

I waited for more, but that was all he said. No hint of what that reason was, and nothing I'd observed so far today had given me any clues either.

"How long is everyone else going to take to get here?" the pacing man asked, his voice rising. "We're not exactly gifted with an abundance of time." He pointed at the general. "You're one of the ones who wanted the kid here, might as well tell him what's going on."

I eased back toward the center of the room. Every instinct told me that this man was not a danger to me. But at the same time, he was clearly agitated and volatile. I didn't want to provoke him.

"Very well, Kramer," said the general. "Bollinger, how familiar are you with the Carpathian Mountains?"

Familiar enough. The range spanned over a thousand miles and ran through central and eastern Europe, crossing a handful of countries. If there was an international incident at play here, the location made sense. "I'm familiar," I said. "Any particular part?"

"Moldova." The single word was supplied by Yang, the quiet man, who was still studying me like he was expecting something more.

I frowned at the general. "A lot of regional tension, given its proximity to Russia and Ukraine. Are we looking at a territorial dispute?"

"A territorial dispute?" Kramer burst out. He rubbed a hand over his face. "No, it's a kidnapping, not a damned land grab."

I kept my expression smooth, but I looked at the general for confirmation, and he nodded. Kidnapping? That *really* wasn't what I'd been expecting.

Behind me, the door opened, and a familiar voice intruded. "Sorry I'm late. You know how traffic can be around DC."

Turning, I found another surprise, but this one truly shook me. I took pride in the fact that I could remain calm in nearly every situation, but clearly this wasn't ordinary.

My uncle, Ian DeRose, stood in the doorway, eyes locked on me. He was a former SEAL himself, though he was long retired. He'd been the owner of Zodiac Tactical, a world-renowned security operation, for as long as I'd known him.

Linear Tactical also provided kidnap and rescue services, but Uncle Ian had resources and contacts that no one else could match. If Zodiac was involved, the situation must be dire.

But the part of the puzzle that didn't fit was *me*. I had no extraordinary skills that would make me critical in this kind of crisis. At least no more than any other SEAL. On the list of available operatives, I would be about as far down the list as you could go since I was no longer active duty.

Which, given Uncle Ian's presence, left only one option: this was personal somehow. And that was fucking terrifying.

CHAPTER THREE

ETHAN

I CROSSED to my uncle and gave him a hug. "Didn't expect to see you here. How's the family? Everyone okay? Aunt Wavy?"

He looked me in the eye like he knew I would be watching for a lie, and I was. He smiled, though it wasn't his real one. A polite version of it.

That didn't make me feel better.

"No worries, kid," he said. "The whole Bollinger clan is doing well. Wavy would kick my ass if she knew I was seeing you. I didn't have a chance to tell her."

"Can we get on with it?" came from behind me. Kramer had finally stopped pacing, had his hands on his hips, and glared at Ian and me.

Ian's smile turned icy. "I see you've met Nigel Kramer and Sidney Yang."

"We weren't formally introduced."

"Is there an update, DeRose?" Kramer asked. "Do we have a plan? We've been waiting for the wunderkind here to arrive,

17

not that I've been given any explanation as to why." Kramer turned to General Moss. "Especially when you have the entire fucking Navy at your disposal."

I caught my uncle's gaze and raised an eyebrow, silently asking what the hell was going on. My fear had dissipated when he'd said that everyone was okay, but this still wasn't adding up, and I needed answers.

"Let me bring Ethan up to speed," Ian said, walking over to the large dining table in the adjacent room. "And then we'll discuss the plan."

Kramer threw his hands in the air. "We don't have time for this."

Ian held out a hand. "Nigel, I promise you that taking the time to do this properly—despite how it feels at this moment— is a thousand times better than going in recklessly and without a plan."

He set out a pile of folders on the table and flipped the first one open. There was a picture on top—a young Asian woman.

"This is Susan Yang, twenty-three, Mr. Yang's daughter," Ian said. I could see the resemblance between them. "Mr. Yang is a U.S. Foreign Service officer, and his post is in Malaysia. Ms. Yang has been kidnapped."

That sucked. Kidnapping happened for a myriad of reasons, none of them good. But I didn't know this girl, and nothing about her told me what I was doing here. I kept silent.

Ian flipped open the next folder, and I froze in place. This photo I did recognize. The guy's face was burned into my brain.

"That's my son," Kramer said, not waiting for Ian to give the breakdown. "Russell Kramer. He's twenty-two. Also kidnapped."

This was the guy that Jess had been flirting with the night of her twenty-first birthday two months ago. The guy that had made me question my entire world. And if he was close with Jess and had been kidnapped . . .

My heart started pounding in my ears. I didn't wait for Ian to flip open the last two folders. I did it myself.

There she was, her perfect face staring up at me from what looked like her ID photo. The other photo I knew to be Alena Spence, her best friend.

Kidnapped.

Jess had been *kidnapped*.

Everything around me snapped into focus. Like I was back on active duty and this mission was all that mattered—because it was.

So this was why I was here. Because Ian knew that if there was one person who would do anything in the world to get Jess back, it was me. I would not stop or rest until she was safe.

Information I had dismissed before now whirled in my brain, and I sifted it for anything I could use to help rescue Jess. I didn't have all the intel. I needed to be patient. But that was asking the impossible. Only seconds had passed, but it felt like an eternity. Everything in the room had shifted.

Everything in the *world* had shifted.

When I'd asked about family, Ian had told me that all the *Bollingers* were well. He'd framed it that way on purpose, knowing he couldn't say the *family* was well because Jess was very definitely family.

Now I saw the agitation and the tension in the men in front of me for what it was: worry and panic for their loved ones. The same reaction I was experiencing. I could forgive Kramer's obnoxious comments .

Because why weren't they using the entire fucking Navy to find Jess?

As if this were one of the critical missions I'd been a part of over the years, I forced my mind to quiet. This time, it was much harder. The thought of Jess in the hands of someone with intent to harm her?

I was going to find her, and I was going to bring her back.

"Tell me everything," I said.

My tone had every man in the room snapping their eyes to me, and the atmosphere went still. I met their gazes in turn. Yes, I was a different man than the one who had walked into this house.

I made the connection before Ian could start speaking again. "They're all from the fellowship program, aren't they?"

"Yes," he said. "All four victims are recipients of the Vandercroft Biotechnology Fellowship."

That made sense. Jess had been a part of the program since she was fourteen, brilliant as she was. So all three of her companions were equally intelligent.

"We have confirmation that they decided to go to Constanta Beach in Romania, just off the Black Sea. Tickets confirm that's where they were."

"I've heard of it." Mostly from Jess. It was a common vacation spot for the younger European crowd and generally considered to be a safe location. "We're sure they were kidnapped?" I asked, clinging to some desperate hope that everyone was overreacting. "No chance they're just holed up somewhere and enjoying their vacation out of sight?"

I didn't particularly like the thought of Jess doing anything out of sight with this guy Russell, but I would take it if it meant she was safe.

"Unfortunately, we're sure." Ian opened a laptop to a video clip. "They were last seen eighteen hours ago. We don't know why exactly they went from Constanta Beach to Moldova, but we know they were there."

The grainy security footage showed the group of four walking along a cobblestone sidewalk. There was no sound to the footage but they were obviously chatting, dressed casually.

They were about to cross a street when a car whipped past them and made one of them—Alena, I think—jump back to keep from getting hit. They all laughed at the close call, so caught up in the adrenaline that they didn't see the van pull up behind them.

It happened in seconds. The van stopped, all doors opened, and masked men swarmed out. It was perfectly timed and executed. These guys were professionals.

Jess was the last one grabbed. I could see her on the video, identifiable by her bright blonde hair. She'd fought back, getting a couple hits in before another guy came back to help. I almost smiled through my gritted teeth, proud that it took more than one of them to force her into that van.

But that almost-smile faded as she took a blow to the face from one of the kidnappers. My hands curled into fists, and rage bubbled through my veins.

The punch didn't stop her. She used every bit of training she'd learned from living around the Linear Tactical guys over the years. But even if she'd managed to get away from these two, she still would've been outnumbered.

The van pulled away smoothly, and they were gone.

I tried to swallow past the fear that closed around my throat as the van drove out of sight of the security camera. I knew, just as Jess had—which was why she'd been fighting so damned hard—that once she was in the van and taken, her chances of survival went down significantly.

No. I refused to even entertain that thought.

"Any other video?" I forced out.

Ian shook his head. "Not much. A few shots to give us a direction on the van, but barely anything. We're lucky we got this. The pickup may have been planned. The visibility is too perfect. Maybe the kidnappers wanted us to see the kids taken so that we'd be prepared for whatever ransom they're going to demand."

"What we don't know," General Moss said, "is why they were taken."

Ian nodded. "It's a perfect storm of reasons."

"Expertise?" I asked.

"That's one," the general admitted. "Political leverage over Yang here is another."

"And your son?" I raised an eyebrow at Kramer.

"Not only is Russell brilliant enough to be part of the fellowship, our family comes from money." He began pacing again.

Ransom from a billionaire was more than enough motive. I didn't have to say aloud that Jess also came from money. Ian and I both knew. Her father was a former country music superstar. Cade Conner. It didn't matter that he no longer performed; he was still a household name all over the world. Her parents had done a pretty decent job of minimizing the public connection for Jess's sake, but it wasn't too hard to find if you were looking.

Jess's friend Alena was a blank spot. No family represented here, so probably no political or financial bigwigs in her closet.

Ian followed my gaze to her photo. "Nothing there yet. No obvious monetary connections, but we're still looking into it."

"Any chance this was random?" I asked. "Like we said, Moldova is pretty damned unstable. Maybe the kidnappers saw a group of Americans, decided to give it a shot, and they don't know that they've gotten lucky?"

"It's a possibility," Ian said after a moment of silence. "But my gut says it wasn't random."

My gut was saying that, too, but it would be far simpler if it were random.

"Either way," General Moss said, crossing his arms, "we want a plan in place before any demands come through."

"You need a SEAL team then," I said. "This would be an easy job for a full team."

I didn't miss his slight wince. "That's not an option at the moment. Relations with Moldova and the surrounding nations are tenuous at best. The US can't send in any official teams and risk those relationships for civilian assets. Private sector only for now, which is where Zodiac Tactical comes into it."

"We have a team ready." Ian crossed his arms over his chest. "Wheels up in two hours. I need you on that team."

I gave him a look. "Did you think there was a chance in hell that I wouldn't be on that plane after you showed me her picture?"

The corners of his mouth tipped up for a moment. "No."

He tapped out something on his phone, and the front door opened. Two men I didn't recognize entered but were clearly expected. "Mr. Yang, Mr. Kramer, my associates are going to go over everything again and make sure that we've gotten everything we need, double-check we haven't missed anything that will help the team get your children back."

They split off to talk to the men, and Ian pulled me back into the living room, General Moss following. Ian put his hand on my shoulder. "Are you all right?"

Was I okay? No. I wasn't. I was desperately forcing my mind to focus on the task at hand and not on the fact that Jess could be scared, hurt, or worse. I was trying not to imagine all the ways that things could go horribly wrong in this situation. But I didn't need to be okay, I just needed to be focused. This was the mission now.

"I'm going to get her back."

Ian nodded. "I don't doubt it."

I turned my back so no one in the other room could hear. "Why don't you tell me why I'm really here? You could get anyone for this mission. Better people than me. And I'm not stupid enough to think that my relationship with Jess isn't a drawback."

You never sent people on missions like this when they were

23

involved with the victims. They couldn't think clearly, and that kind of emotion caused bad decisions. Not that I was going to allow that to happen.

Ian sighed and looked at the general, who nodded. There was more. I'd known that from the beginning.

"This is a lot more complicated than we're letting them know." Ian kept his voice quiet.

"How?"

General Moss rubbed the back of his neck. "One of the four people who was taken is a traitor."

I stared at him. "What?"

"Research was stolen from the lab at Vandercroft right before the four of them left on vacation," Ian said. "Critical research. The kind of thing we don't want in enemy hands."

Fuck. That changed things.

Moss and Ian shot a look at each other.

"What?" I asked. I needed all the info.

Ian's hand fell onto my shoulder. "We don't have confirmation but . . . right now it looks like Jess is the traitor."

I shrugged his hand off. "No. No way in hell. You really think that Jess is a traitor?"

Ian shook his head. "Of course not. But I have to look at what's in front of me. And right now, that's where the evidence is pointing. You and I both know that things like this are never as simple as they appear."

"Could she be under coercion?"

The general nodded. "We've talked about that. It's possible. And Kramer and Yang both have pasts that make us cautious. It's not out of the question that their kids are responsible. Ultimately, the important thing is recovering the stolen data. Lives are at stake in a very literal way."

"I'm assuming you're not going to tell me why," I said.

General Moss shook his head. "Clearance."

I nodded. When I'd been on active duty, our SEAL team

hadn't always had clearance to understand everything about our mission. So not getting top secret info now was to be expected.

But damn, I wanted it. Even tangential information could be useful in a situation like this. It could predict how people thought. Could save lives. Could save *Jess*.

"General?" One of Ian's employees called him over to speak with Kramer, leaving me and Ian alone.

"You know Jess wouldn't do this," I said. "I'm getting her out, but I won't be a part of proving her guilty."

Ian shook his head. "I know. Get her out and recover the data. I didn't call you in to haul Jess to jail, and I would never let that happen. But that's a bridge we'll have to cross later."

Good. We were on the same page.

I nodded and headed back over to the table with the files so I could memorize more details. I didn't have much time.

Jess stared up at me from her photo, and even though I should be looking at everything else, I couldn't take my eyes off the picture. I'd loved her my entire life. She'd crashed into my world when she was four years old, and we'd been together ever since. It had always been the two of us.

I breathed around the heaviness in my chest and through the fear. She was out there and in danger. And from more than just the kidnappers, it sounded like.

Jess, what have you gotten yourself into?

CHAPTER FOUR

EIGHT YEARS Ago
   Ethan - 16
   Jess - 13

"I'M READY, Ethan. I'm ready for you to kiss me."

This would have been much more exciting if it were Ethan standing here in her arms, rather than Jess holding a mango.

She'd wanted to practice and the internet had said to take a soft fruit, like a mango or a plum, and cut out a small hole the size of a mouth. That way, she could get an understanding of what Ethan's lips would feel like pressed up against hers when he finally kissed her.

What his tongue would feel like.

She wanted the first kiss with Ethan to be perfect. She needed to practice so she wouldn't seem like such a newbie. Ethan would be great at kissing, but Ethan was great at everything. She didn't want him to kiss her and be disappointed because she didn't know what she was doing.

Plus, she liked research. Liked learning. Liked trial and

JANE CROUCH

error and precise methodology. So this mango was about to become her independent variable.

She brought the sweet fruit up to her lips. It was soft. Ethan's lips would be soft too. She moved her mouth around to get used to the feel, and then slowly slipped her tongue into the hole she'd cut out in the mango. She pressed her face more firmly against it—wanting to experience it so she would know what to expect.

"Oh, Ethan," she said, pushing her mouth more firmly against the fruit.

"What in the hell is going on?"

Jess dropped the mango from her face and spun, mortified at the sound of her father's voice behind her.

"I—" She didn't know what to say that could possibly make this less embarrassing. "I—"

"What were you doing to that poor fruit?" her father asked.

"Cade—" Jess's mother held out a hand to stop Dad from talking. Ethan stood next to them, holding little Ella's hand, staring at Jess.

Jess wanted to melt into the ground. Ethan had witnessed her making out with a piece of fruit too.

The mango fell from her limp hand onto the ground, and Jess turned and ran. She heard everyone calling after her, but she didn't stop.

She wanted to die. She had never been so embarrassed in her entire life. She ran all the way up to her bedroom and locked the door, but she couldn't stay here. Mom and Dad would be knocking any second.

She ran over to her window, yanked it open, and climbed out onto a branch of the red maple tree outside it like she had dozens of times before. She clambered down and ran for the barn, then behind it. She wiped tears of mortification from her eyes as she climbed up a stack of hay bales.

How could she have gotten caught doing something so

28

stupid? Mom, Dad, and Ella weren't supposed to get home for another hour. They must have seen Ethan in town and brought him over.

And the fact that Ethan had seen her doing that . . . she wanted to die. She would never be able to face any of them again, especially Ethan.

She rolled onto her side and clutched her stomach. Normally, she loved lying out on the hay bales and watching the Wyoming sky, but not today.

"Room for one more up there?"

She wrapped her arms more tightly around herself at the sound of Ethan's voice. "Go away. I can't talk about this."

"Come on, Jess. It's me. We can talk about anything. Are you really that embarrassed that you were mangling a mango?"

He was getting closer, climbing up the bales. She didn't have the heart to turn him away. She would never have the heart to turn Ethan away. But she couldn't face him either. She rolled so her back was to him.

"You know I wasn't just eating the mango. Don't act like you don't know that."

"Then let's talk about what you were doing with the mango. There's nothing you and I can't talk about."

She squeezed her eyes shut. He was right. There had never been anything the two of them hadn't talked about.

He'd been the one she'd called last year, panicking when her first period had started at school and she'd needed to get home to change clothes. He'd ditched his high school classes and driven her.

She could tell Ethan anything. She sat up and glanced at him.

"I was kissing the mango."

He didn't laugh at her admission. He just sat there, his body language mimicking hers, his arms wrapped around his knees.

"Research?" he asked.

She looked over at him, surprised. "How did you know?"

Now he chuckled. "Jess, it's you. You're always doing some sort of experiment. If you were kissing a piece of fruit, it was either to find out which was softest or sweetest or something."

"It was to practice kissing," she said. "I read in an article that if you were nervous about kissing, you could practice with a piece of fruit, and that would give you an idea of what someone's lips and tongue would feel like."

"Oh." Now he seemed a little more surprised.

"I wanted our first kiss to be perfect."

He ran a hand through his thick, dark hair. "Our first kiss will be perfect. I know it. Every kiss we have will be perfect. There's no hurry. We have forever."

Jess slammed her fist down on the hay. "Everybody else my age has already kissed somebody. Simone Wheeler was talking about making out with Jonah Littleman behind the tennis courts the other day, and they don't really like each other! People kiss all the time in the hallway at school even though it's not allowed. I'm the only one who hasn't kissed anyone, and I've had a boyfriend for the longest time."

"Jess—" He reached a hand out, but she jerked back.

"I know, I know, you're perfect, and you'll wait until I'm forty years old and we're married before you kiss me for the first time. I'm not a kid anymore, Ethan! I'm thirteen, and I love you, and I want my first kiss to be with—"

She broke off as his hands cupped her cheeks and pulled her close, his mouth falling on hers.

This was so much better than a mango.

It was everything she'd always dreamed her first kiss with Ethan would be. His lips were firm, but gentle, just a little bit hesitant. His tongue, when it brushed against hers, was so much sweeter than any fruit could ever be.

Perfect.

CHAPTER FIVE

Jess

HORROR MOVIES HAD NEVER SCARED me, even when I was little. It had become a kind of game among my friends and family to find one that would spook me, but no one had ever been able to.

The films were filled with people making irrational decisions and completely oblivious to all the escape options around them. I had yet to see a movie where the masked villain or monster had come up with a way of attacking the protagonist that couldn't have been avoided with basic geometry. The angles of their assaults were overly simple, and equally simple to dodge or sidestep at the right moment and escape unharmed.

Other people never seemed to think that it was as straight-forward as I did. And more than once, I'd ruined movies for people because I'd pointed out flaws in the logic of the story or setup. But through all that, I had never been scared.

Now I was scared, and this was anything but simple.

I wasn't scared only because I was in a tiny dark room. Or only because I was chained so tightly to the floor that I couldn't stand up all the way.

It wasn't just because I'd been punched in the face and thrown into a van, either. Or even because every person I'd seen here was armed to the teeth with guns that were meant for a battlefield.

No, I was scared because I had created a situation that I'd thought I could control. And it was now clear that I couldn't.

Maybe thinking about horror movies was a comfort because they weren't real, and they weren't scary.

This situation was both.

It wasn't supposed to have happened this way. Nobody was supposed to have gotten hurt.

As if the universe could read my thoughts, a scream rang out nearby. Begging. Pleading that was silenced by the muffled sound of someone being beaten.

Alena.

She'd been my best friend for the past couple of years in the Vandercroft Biotechnology Fellowship program. The women there were outnumbered ten to one, so finding someone relatively close to my age had been a godsend. I couldn't just do nothing while they tortured her.

I hauled in a breath and put everything behind my voice. "Leave her alone!"

The sound echoed off the walls of the tiny room, and for the thousandth time I yanked on the bonds holding me. My wrists were raw from pulling against the metal.

And even though I knew I didn't have the angle to leverage my strength against the metal chains and escape, I still pulled again. The sound of my friend screaming threw my rational brain out the window.

The door slammed open, bouncing off the wall from the force used. "Quiet," a heavily accented voice said.

I couldn't see his face. He was silhouetted in the light from the hallway, plus my eyes were blind from the total darkness in here.

His English was broken, but he still got the point across. "You want scream too? Quiet."

"Leave her alone," I said. "She hasn't done anything. None of us have. What do you want?"

My vision cleared enough to see that he, too, carried a huge gun. The casual way his hand rested on it told me he was comfortable using it and wouldn't mind using it on me.

Someone yelled at him from down the hall, a guttural language that I didn't quite recognize. It wasn't Romanian. I scanned through my brain, trying to match the dialect. Maybe it was Gagauz?

I mentally kicked myself for not brushing up on more of the local dialects before taking this trip. I hadn't thought it would matter, definitely not like this, and I'd thrown myself into my work instead.

If I'd sat down for a couple days and brushed up, maybe I wouldn't be straining, trying to match up parts of speech and Germanic roots to piece together anything useful from what people were saying.

"Please," I said again, ignoring his warning. "Leave my friend alone and let us go."

He walked closer. Maybe I had a chance to reason with him. "Please. If you'll just let us go—"

"I told you, quiet!"

His boot kicked out toward me. I twisted just enough to take the blow on my hip rather than my ribs. I didn't need a medical degree to know a blow of that force would've definitely cracked a rib. I cried out as he kicked at me a second time, hitting my thigh full force.

"Quiet!" Then he spat out what I assumed was a curse and left me in darkness again.

I hauled in a breath through the pain radiating up my side, gritting my teeth. I kept my breathing even until the pain subsided enough to think again.

The hip hurt like a bitch but was much better than taking a boot to the ribs, which would've completely hindered any thoughts of escape, not that there seemed to be many escape options.

Growing up around the Linear Tactical guys, my extended family who'd all been in the Special Forces, meant that I'd watched and participated in more self-defense classes before finishing elementary school than most people did their entire lives. I knew to protect the most vulnerable parts of myself like my head and ribs.

But that knowledge didn't stop my hip and thigh from hurting like a mother. I was going to have boot-shaped bruises within the hour.

I wished I had one of those Special Forces guys with me right now. They'd know exactly how to handle this situation. Any of them . . . Uncle Zac, Uncle Finn, Uncle Gavin. Even my dad, who didn't have any Special Forces background, would be helpful. Growing up in Wyoming taught you a lot of survival skills.

But I really wanted Ethan.

As always.

But no. I put him out of my mind. I might want him here with me, but I didn't want him in this situation. He might be a SEAL, but as a medic—and a brilliant one at that—he wasn't going to be much help against these thugs. I hoped to God we wouldn't need his kind of skill here. But given the scream I'd heard, I wasn't so sure.

Shifting so there was less pressure on my bruising leg, I closed my eyes. The pain of missing Ethan was much worse than that of my leg, right now especially.

We'd had to be apart so much the past few years—he was in

the Navy, and I was in London. But we'd made it work. The distance had always been temporary in light of our forever. It had never occurred to us *not* to make it work.

Until a couple of months ago.

I should have reached out and talked to him before I tried to do something this stupid.

Or if I hadn't told him, I should have at least seen him. Kissed him. Held him. But I hadn't done that. Because even though I was a genius, I was also the world's biggest idiot.

I'd been giving him the cold shoulder for two months because I was angry that he'd missed my birthday. My twenty-first. Of course, I'd known that he couldn't come—he'd been on a mission or something where he couldn't give me the details. And those were good reasons.

But he hadn't called. In the seventeen years we'd known each other, Ethan had never missed reaching out to me on one of my birthdays. I couldn't pretend that it didn't sting.

And then I'd been all wrapped up in this *brilliant* plan and told myself it was fine if there was some distance between us.

I'd been so wrong.

I should have called him and confronted him about missing my birthday. Gotten that out in the open, even if I couldn't tell him about the rest. I should've called him an ass —something I'd definitely done before—and been done with it. Then at least I'd have known he was mine again. My Ethan.

Instead, I'd made shitty choices that had led me here. God, I missed him.

If I got out of here, I was never letting anything so stupid come between the two of us again. Ethan was worth it. The grudge wasn't.

The door slammed open again, and I couldn't help but flinch away, but this time the guard wasn't alone. Alena, hands bound, was pushed into the room before the door pulled closed and the lock slid home. She stumbled and tried to catch herself and was only marginally successful.

"Alena," I said, moving as close to her as I could. "Oh my gosh, are you okay?"

"Jess."

Her whisper was fractured. Rough and broken. The dim light in the room showed me that I was right. She'd been beaten. Her nose was bloody and her eye was darkening. When she moved toward me, she favored her right leg and gasped as she lowered herself to the ground.

It could have been worse. That was a screwed-up thing to say, but on the surface, at least there was no permanent damage. How long it would stay that way for any of us was an entirely different story.

"How badly are you hurt? Did they tell you what they want?" I reached out, helping to settle her against the wall near me as best I could.

"Money," she said softly, her head sagging against the wall. "They said they wanted money. I tried to tell them that we're students and that we didn't have any money. They didn't seem to believe me, but I tried."

Her eyes closed, and I hesitated. The loyalty Alena had shown me even though she was in pain meant everything to me. Because she'd lied. Alena didn't have money, but I did. My family was rich because of my father's music career. Susan and Russell also came from wealthy families. The people who had taken us could ask for a ransom and get millions of dollars without even breaking a sweat.

But Alena hadn't used that to her advantage. It would have been so easy for her to point a finger in our direction and tell our captors we were the ones they wanted. But she hadn't.

Reaching out, I took her hand. She squeezed back just a little, eyes still closed.

"Did you see Susan? Or Russell?"

Alena shook her head. "For like a second in a room down the hall." She swallowed. "The kidnappers don't seem very organized. Even when they were—" She cut off like the words were too hard. "There were times it felt like they didn't really know what to do with me. I got the feeling that they're filling time until someone else gets here."

"What makes you say that?"

She opened her eyes and looked at me. "They kept arguing. One wanted to hit me more but the other stopped him, gesturing toward the door."

"I'm so sorry, Alena."

"What if they're only keeping us alive until their boss gets here, Jess?"

I bit my lip. "I don't know. If they wanted to kill us, they could have done that already. But they haven't." My mind scrambled to make all the pieces fit, but they didn't. Not yet. "Were they asking you questions or anything? Was there something they wanted to know?"

"No," Alena said. "They told me that they wanted money. That we would pay. They don't speak English that well."

Then why hurt her like that? To make the rest of us more pliable when they used us to ask for ransom? Purely as a threat to keep us scared so that we wouldn't attempt to escape?

Alena closed her eyes, slumping against the wall. I didn't ask her anything else. She'd been through enough, and the best thing she could do right now was sleep.

But if she was right, and we were being held here until someone else came for us, then we needed to get out now.

Think, Jess. You've solved harder problems than this.

The walls surrounding me were stone. Rough and old. The floor too. Based on the style and the state of it, the building was probably over a hundred years old. In the time I'd been here, I hadn't heard any signs of civilization. Just some sheep and maybe a cow.

So we were in the country. Maybe an abandoned or forcibly occupied farm. They had drugged us in the van, so I had no idea how long we'd driven or if longer than a day had passed since we'd been taken. My body had been stiff and sore when I'd woken up in this room. So I was guessing at least twelve hours, but that didn't help.

The only thing I could verify was that we were somewhere in the countryside on what seemed like an old farm. Not exactly something that would narrow it down.

Even if we were hours from the nearest city, we needed to get out soon. Now I had a problem to solve. Better than sitting here doing nothing. I shifted into a more comfortable position to accommodate the chains and let my mind go to work.

CHAPTER SIX

ETHAN

THREE HOURS TO GO. I'd been counting down every hour on the hour since waking up. It was a twelve-hour flight from DC to Moldova, and once we put wheels down, there wouldn't be much time for sleep.

So I'd forced myself to sleep, or at least put myself into a state of conserving physical and mental energy, a trick I'd learned as a SEAL.

It was harder this time, knowing the mission centered around the most important part of my world. But I would do anything for Jess. If that meant conserving my energy now so I was at full strength once we hit the ground, I'd do that too, hard as it might be.

And it was hard. The adrenaline in my system, surging from thinking about what Jess could be going through, demanded an outlet. I could drop and do two hundred pushups or run ten miles and still have plenty of energy leftover.

My body had one goal: get my woman to safety. It didn't understand the wait.

But my mind controlled my body. So I locked that shit down and forced myself to rest. My body would get the chance to do what it wanted once there was an enemy to face.

At least the private jet Ian had provided was comfortable, far more luxurious than any military transport I'd ever flown in. That helped with the resting. Flying twelve hours on a thin metal seat with earplugs shoved in, as was the life of a SEAL, made relaxing harder.

The rest of the team was toward the front of the plane, including two other former SEALs, Landon Black and Isaac Baxter. They were a good deal older than me, but they were in good shape, and I had no doubt they could hold their own. And they came with Ian's recommendation. He'd worked with both of them a long time.

I trusted Uncle Ian with my life. And that was what was at stake here. My life. Because Jess was my life. Ian wouldn't send anyone he didn't think was capable of doing this job.

Forcing my thoughts away from Jess, I closed my eyes. But that didn't help. When I shut them, I imagined the worst that could be happening to her. Injury, torture, and darker, viler things. Just the thoughts made my vision tint red and my knuckles go white around the plane's armrests. They nearly creaked with the strain.

She was fine.

She had to be fine.

I wasn't going to lose her before I'd had an opportunity to tell her that I was hers. Wholly and completely. I thought she'd known, but these past two months, I'd been more distant, biding my time as I worked out my plan . . .

Nothing was more important than getting her to safety so I could win her back properly. I wanted to sink into her and never come up for air. The second I found her, I'd be tempted to wrap Jess in my arms and never let go, even when we needed to move quickly.

And that was the reason they didn't send entangled people on missions like this. I needed to keep myself in check. I would keep myself in check.

Survival first. Always.

Everything else, including dragging Jess to the nearest bed and making love to her until we couldn't figure out where one of us ended and the other began, had to be secondary.

I stood, stretching my legs, looking back at the others. The fourth man on the team was a mystery. Harold MacQueen. Nigel Kramer had insisted on his presence on the mission. The entire time we'd stayed at that house in Falls Church, Kramer hadn't calmed down for a second. By the time we'd left for the airfield, I'd been worried he was going to blow an artery.

MacQueen had shown up just before we were about to leave, and there'd been something about him from the get-go I hadn't liked. Nothing obvious, just a gut feeling. Ian had had the same one, pulling me aside as we got on the jet and letting me know he was gathering more intel on MacQueen.

But unless we got confirmation he was working against us, we'd have to trust him to a degree. It was going to take all four of us to get the hostages out safely.

Ian had wanted to be part of the mission, too, but had benched himself because of old injuries. Plus, he was more useful making sure we got the intel we needed.

"Ethan," Isaac's voice reached me from the front of the plane, "got some more info."

I walked back and joined them around the table. Frankly, I wasn't used to planes having tables, but it was easier than crouching over crumpled maps.

And we weren't looking at paper. We were looking at a large tablet showing a portion of the Moldovan countryside. "Most recent intel has the hostages here." Isaac pointed to a spot on the screen. "It's a mill. Been empty for a decade, but there are some nearby farms."

"What places them there?"

"Satellites mostly," Landon answered. "There was surveillance in the area, and it caught the path of the van."

I raised my eyebrows, surprised. "That's lucky."

Landon smiled grimly. "It was lucky that they caught the van's path, but I've heard of stranger things. Most of eastern Europe is under satellite surveillance. Which is good for us."

"Yeah," I said. "Good to not go in blind. Good to have anything at all."

MacQueen sighed. "But that's where the good news ends."

I looked at Isaac. I wanted my news from him or Landon, not MacQueen.

"Unfortunately, he's right. That mill has a lot of tactical advantages, definitely why they chose it. It's on high ground, and from what we can gather, the walls are stone. It's well built and they've got defenses set up."

Isaac brought up a slightly blurry image—a top-down view of the location—and pointed to what looked like mounted guns. "The location is easily defensible. And since they're surrounded by active farms, it's less suspicious than being somewhere completely isolated."

I scrubbed my hand through my cropped hair, poring through all the information I had and trying to make it fit. An all-out assault wouldn't work. We would need stealth and a surprise if we were going to do it. "Anything going for us?"

Landon nodded. "One thing. Looks like it's a skeleton crew."

They wouldn't need a lot of manpower when they had so many other tactical advantages.

Isaac leaned back in his seat. "Here's what we're thinking. Nothing fancy. We'll leave the vehicles a couple miles down the road to avoid detection. We've got tranquilizer guns. Strike after nightfall, tranq everyone in sight, and walk in the front door."

Everyone sitting at this table knew that it probably wouldn't be that simple, but I agreed it was the best plan given the circumstances.

"Injuries could be a complication," I pointed out. "If anyone isn't mobile, moving them two miles could be tricky."

Once again, I had to lock down my mind, refusing to think about Jess broken and bleeding. That she might be alone and terrified. My girl was strong as hell, but any soldier knew everyone broke under the right circumstances.

Was she afraid for her life? Was she wondering if she'd be rescued?

My chest felt tight, rage bubbling up. Every thought made me want to rip a hole in the side of the damn plane.

Lock it down, Bollinger. Save it for the fight.

"Yes, injuries are a factor," Isaac agreed. "We'll have to work that as we come to it."

I nodded.

"Anything else?" MacQueen stood. "I've got to go to the bathroom."

Isaac shook his head. As soon as the door closed behind MacQueen, Isaac and Landon turned to me.

"We think MacQueen is here because of the research," Landon said.

"How so?"

Isaac tapped the tablet and brought up a report on MacQueen, turning it toward me so I could read it. "Ian hasn't been able to find anything on him. He's a little too clean, which sends up red flags for us. It's possible that Kramer has sent him because he knows his son Russell stole the research, or because he had his son steal the research."

"But no proof," I said.

"No." Isaac sighed. "But all the same, we think it's a good

idea to keep an eye on MacQueen and Russell, when we find him."

I nodded. Finding proof Russell Kramer was the thief would make my life easier in more ways than one. Most importantly, it would prove Jess was innocent. Then the guy she'd been flirting with would be an international criminal and on his way to prison for the foreseeable future. That helped greatly with the wooing-her-back plan.

Landon crossed his arms over his chest. "Because if he's not the guilty party, and Jess is—"

"She's not." The words snapped out of my mouth like a whip, and he held up a hand.

"I don't think she is either, but it would be stupid of us not to be prepared for the possibility. So we need to tell you about the secondary mission if that happens."

I clenched my jaw in an effort not to insist there was no need for a secondary mission because Jess wasn't guilty. She couldn't be. It ran contrary to everything I knew about her as a person.

Of course, the past couple of months . . . was I really even sure I knew everything about her anymore? Could she have been deceived into doing something stupid?

Landon watched me carefully, like I was some wild animal who might turn and attack him any second. It wasn't terribly far from the truth. "Returning the research is top priority. I don't know what the data is, but it has been made clear that it *cannot* fall into the wrong hands."

"What is it?" I managed, my voice rough.

He shook his head. "I honestly don't know. Above my clearance. But it is top priority, even over the rescue of the hostages."

I scrubbed a hand over my face. "That's not going to work for me. And if Jess is involved, I won't just turn her over."

Isaac's hand fell on my shoulder. "If the worst happens and

Jess is guilty, Ian has a backup plan. We have instructions to get you both out of the country and set up someplace where Jess can't be prosecuted. And you'll be there to make sure she's safe and protected. Forever."

I sucked in a breath. Ian had really thought this through. If he had already set up this kind of contingency, it was more than serious. It was life and death. This was the kind of thing you didn't come back from.

And evidence must really point at Jess being guilty.

I would do it, of course. I would run with Jess anywhere in the world and make sure we stayed out of sight for the rest of our lives if that was what was needed. Even if that meant we'd never see any of our family again. Or the United States.

Jess had always been—and always would be—my priority.

I'd spent a big chunk of my life protecting Jess. She could be wild and reckless and completely unaware of her own limitations. It was one of the things I loved about her.

It also meant that sometimes she needed to be protected from herself. I never imagined that this would be one of the ways I would have to do that. But I would.

I had decided a long time ago that every breath I took would be dedicated to making Jess safe and happy. What I'd found out in the past few hours didn't change that.

"I understand," I said. "But that's not going to be necessary. I promise."

They shared a look that told me they weren't quite convinced. But I was.

"Good," Isaac said. "But I expect you to tell us if it becomes necessary."

I nodded again. "I will. I won't put her in danger."

We stopped talking as the bathroom door opened and MacQueen rejoined us at the table. "Should we plan out our offensive for once we're on the ground?"

45

I made room so he could sit next to me at the table. "Let's do it."

We only had a couple hours until go time, and we needed to finalize every detail and examine as many variables as possible to try to eliminate problems before they happened.

So that's what we did. MacQueen was surprisingly helpful, looking at the situation from different angles than the rest of us, who all had the same SEAL training. By the time we hit the airfield an hour away from our target, we had a solid plan in hand.

Everything we needed was on the plane already, and as we descended, we armed ourselves. No more than what we could carry on our bodies with backup bags in the car. Tranq guns with ammo and silenced handguns for an absolute emergency. Anything larger would be too noticeable.

"Ethan," Landon called as I was putting dark paint on my skin, "review it for us one more time."

I wasn't offended. This was standard protocol. Each of us would take turns repeating the plan out loud so we were sure we were all not only on the same page, but on the same line and the same word on that page.

"Circle around to the north and climb the rocks on the back side. Tranq the guard on our synced count. Through the door or window and clear the northeast corner. Search for hostages. Rendezvous at the vehicles."

He had the others recite their paths, and he repeated his as well. There were no flaws. We were ready.

As we deplaned and jumped into the waiting cars, steely calm overtook me. I was familiar with the sensation, the way my mind collapsed everything else but what was in front of me. There was only the mission. Nothing else mattered. Nothing else existed. But this time, the end of the mission was Jess.

No mission had ever mattered this much.

CHAPTER SEVEN

Two Months Ago
  Ethan - 24
  Jess - 21

"You here to tour around, mate? You're an American, right?"

Ethan met his cab driver's eyes in the rearview mirror. "Not really touring. Here to visit a friend for her birthday."

He wasn't in uniform, and he only had forty hours of leave before he had to be back in Germany to meet up with the rest of his SEAL team. He hadn't been sure he'd be able to take these two days. It had looked like they were going to be sent out on an emergency mission, but the situation had taken care of itself at the last moment.

He'd thought this was the first birthday of Jess's since meeting her that he was going to have to miss. That had never happened so far, and he was glad to not end the streak on her twenty-first.

He might actually pull off surprising his little genius.

As far as she knew, because that was what he'd thought was going to happen, his team was somewhere in northern Africa. His last brief communication with her three days ago had been to tell her he wasn't going to make it.

Jess had been disappointed but had understood Ethan couldn't always be there. At this point, with them both having hectic careers, they were well familiar with the ins and outs of a long-distance relationship. They did their best to see each other as often as they could and still managed to talk nearly every day unless Ethan was on an active mission.

But he couldn't wait to see the surprise in Jess's eyes when he showed up. And he had one more surprise too: the ring in his jacket pocket.

He'd had it for a while now, but it was time. They were both ready. He had to make a decision in the next few weeks about whether to re-up in the Navy or get out.

The ring in his pocket said it was time to get out. There was a lot he could do in the private sector with skills he'd developed in the military that would serve him well. But most importantly, he just wanted to be with Jess.

"Is your girl from Britain then?" the cabbie asked.

"She's studying here. She's lived in London for seven years now. So I've been here quite a few times."

"And does she know you're coming? This club we're headed to is quite popular. Might be hard to find her."

"No, she doesn't know I'm here," Ethan said. "I wasn't sure I was going to make it and didn't want to get her hopes up if I couldn't."

"Big surprise?" The cab driver waggled his eyebrows.

"I hope so," Ethan answered, "and I hope to make it even more romantic by the end of the night. I've got an important question to ask her. *The* important question."

"Well then, I hope she says yes, mate." The cabbie was grinning as they pulled up in front of the club. "Good luck to you."

"Thank you." Ethan got out of the cab, paid the driver, and went inside. He didn't have a bag—he had some stuff stashed at Jess's apartment. All he needed was to find her.

The place was big, crowded, and smoky. The bass of the music was so loud he felt it in his chest. It was going to take a while to find Jess. Fortunately, he was good at reconnaissance missions.

It only took him ten seconds to realize this place definitely wasn't where he wanted to propose to her. When he found her, maybe he could talk her into leaving. But maybe she was with friends for a proper celebration.

And maybe he wanted to do more than just get down on one knee and ask her. Damn it. He should have thought this through.

People did all sorts of elaborate proposals nowadays, but hell, he and Jess had been talking about getting married since she was four years old. This latest conversation would merely be the one that made it official.

He wanted to start a life with her, one where they lived in the same place all the time and woke up in the same bed every morning. He was ready. Of course, he'd been ready for fourteen years.

He knew the moment he was in the same vicinity as Jess. It had been this way his whole life. He wasn't one to wax poetic. He wasn't good with fancy love words. But when he was near her, there was something in her soul that called to his. Soulmates.

She was out on the dance floor with her friends, smiling and laughing and jumping around. He walked over to the bar and ordered a beer. He'd never been much for dancing, but he always liked to drink in the sight of Jess O'Conner.

A couple of ladies tried to engage him in conversation, but

he gave them a polite smile and turned his attention back to Jess. He wasn't here for anyone else, wasn't interested in anyone else.

A few minutes later when the music turned slower, instead of coming off the dance floor, Jess went into the arms of one of the people she was with. Ethan took one last sip of his beer. A slow dance, he didn't mind cutting in on. He wanted Jess in his arms.

But as he watched, things turned sideways.

Why was she dancing so close to this guy? Why was her hand threaded in his hair at the back of his neck?

Ethan wasn't aggressive by nature. He was calm, level-headed, and tended to think through possible scenarios before jumping to any sort of judgment or plan. But right now, it was all Ethan could do not to walk over there and leave the guy unconscious on the ground. He knew a dozen ways to make it happen without breaking a sweat.

He slid his beer away. He didn't want anything hampering his judgment. He was on full alert, details clarifying around him. Like when he was on a mission.

And then he waited.

He waited as the guy twirled Jess around and she laughed. He waited as the guy continued to dance with her when the slow song was over. He waited for the next two hours while Jess danced and smiled and flirted.

This guy wasn't a stranger to her. He was one of her colleagues, one of her friends. Ethan didn't recognize him the way he did the others in her group, but the guy had the same nerdy look as the others. Jess was the only one who somehow managed to pull off brilliant, fun, and down to earth all at the same time.

Watching them was torture and yet . . . not. Because while Ethan definitely didn't like seeing Jess flirt with this guy—

touching him, standing close to him, laughing with him—there wasn't any one moment where she crossed a line.

She didn't kiss him. Didn't rub up against him inappropriately. Didn't do anything that she would have to confess.

The longer Ethan watched, the more it seemed like the entire evening was some sort of experiment. Not surprising. Research with strict methodology was how her brain worked.

But what exactly was she researching now?

What it would be like to be with someone who wasn't Ethan? Was she testing the waters to see if she liked it?

Ethan scrubbed a hand over his face as Jess and her mystery man went back out on the dance floor for another slow dance. All Ethan did was watch.

His whole life, he'd only had one real concern when it came to him and Jess. He'd always known he would spend forever with her. That he was hers. But knowing *when* their forever should start had been a little trickier.

Ethan was all Jess had ever known romantically.

As he watched her with this guy now, the slightly awkward movements between them, the ring in his pocket mocked him.

Maybe he was too early. Maybe Jess needed a chance to go out and know other guys. As much as that would rip his heart to shreds, he was willing to stand by and let her do whatever she needed to do.

He could lose a battle in order to win the war, but he also knew that was dangerous. He was gone so much of the time in the Navy. Maybe she was tired of waiting. Maybe she was ready to be with someone she could go to bed with each night and not have to wait weeks, or months at a time, to see.

Maybe this trip was giving Ethan the exact intel he needed. He shifted back against the bar.

He waited another hour, keeping an eye on her, his mission shifting to one of protection. If Jess wanted this guy, that was her choice, but Ethan wasn't going to let anyone take advantage of her.

As she dumped her drinks and turned down shots, unlike her friends and the guy, Ethan was relieved. She might be experimenting, but at least she was doing it with her full mental resources.

When they finally headed for the club's exit, he followed, staying in the shadows but close enough that he could hear them. It sounded like they were heading back to the Vandercroft campus.

Good. He hoped.

Jess was getting in the cab when she suddenly stopped and turned, looking around. He stepped back so as not to be seen. She obviously wasn't looking for him, but he didn't want her to know he was here.

They'd be having a discussion, but not yet. There were things Ethan had to put into motion first.

He watched the vehicle pull away, then got in the queue for his own taxi. This had not been the night he was expecting.

He got into a taxi and looked up, startled, when the driver gave a surprised yelp. "Hey, mate! I didn't expect to get you as a fare again tonight. How did it go with your lady friend?"

"About how you would expect given I'm without her and the ring is still here in my pocket."

The cabbie winced. "Sorry to hear that. That's never the ending you're hoping for."

"No, definitely not. But now I know where I stand."

The taxi driver was smart enough to realize Ethan didn't want to talk more. And instead of going to the hotel as he'd planned, he had the man take him back to the airport.

He'd been in the Navy for seven years. He'd always known he wasn't a lifer. It had only been a matter of when he would get out and he and Jess could start their life together.

Maybe dancing in somebody else's arms was what she

needed before they started that. If so, Ethan was willing to let her have it.

But ultimately, they would be together, and he would fight for what they had. Hell, he was going to do more than just fight.

He was going to *win*.

CHAPTER EIGHT

Jess

THE SLAMMING SOUND WAS DISORIENTING, and it took three seconds too long for me to remember where I was. In those three seconds, there were hands on me, pulling me up and unlocking the chains from the floor.

I was still kidnapped, still stuck in this tiny hellhole, and I knew one thing for certain: the fact that they were moving us was *not* a good sign.

Those three seconds cost me. I wasn't in a good position to struggle, but I did anyway. I shoved my elbow into the gut of the man who was holding me. Because his hands were on me and not his gun, that gave me just a fraction of an advantage.

And in situations like this, fractions were all you had. He grunted in pain before cursing and pulling me closer, speaking quickly to the man on my other side. I kicked out at them, but it was too late for me to get a good hold. Another curse as I managed to catch a shin with my toe.

The click of a gun froze me. I was hanging from their arms,

off-balance and completely reliant on them to keep me upright. The gun wasn't pointed at me. It was pointed at Alena, jammed up underneath her chin with a force that looked painful.

The guy who had kicked me had her. He'd figured out my weak point when I'd told them to leave her alone. It was a trade I'd make all over again in order to save my friend pain, but that didn't mean I wouldn't be tempted to punch the smug smile off his face if my hands were free.

Calm down, Jess. Focus.

I took a breath and then another. Survival first and foremost. Nobody got rescued if they were dead.

I needed more information. Maybe this change would provide it. Though if they were marching us to our deaths, I would fight like hell again.

The man holding the gun jerked his chin toward the door. "Walk."

The light in the hallway was bright enough to hurt my eyes after so much darkness, but I blinked away the pain in order to look around. They weren't bothering to hide our sight, which wasn't a great sign, but I was going to soak up every detail I could.

There were more of them than I'd thought. In the short hallway they dragged us down, I counted at least a dozen guards. Alena had said there hadn't that been many around, which meant more had arrived. Possibly with whomever the first guys had been waiting for.

That would make sense. Move us now because the boss was here.

The soldiers were armed, though not every weapon was the same. There was a variety, from semi-automatic rifles to simple pistols. So likely not something organized or with enough structure to make things standard issue. No obvious insignia or markings that would give me a clue about who they were or their motivations.

And that was all I could get before we burst through a door into another small, well-lit room. There was a folding table with four chairs, two of them already occupied by Russell and Susan.

They had a few visible bruises, but nothing compared to what our captors had done to Alena. In the light, it was obvious that she'd been beaten. A black eye was forming and her jaw was swelling. In the few seconds before they shoved us into the empty seats, she limped heavily.

No one said anything. I didn't know which of our captors spoke English, and I wasn't about to give them more ammunition to use against us, so I kept quiet.

The door swung open, and a man entered. He was better dressed than the rest of the soldiers, and he carried himself with an air of authority. So the boss had arrived. The other soldiers cringed away from him like they were afraid, averting their eyes.

This was the man who was going to decide if we lived or died.

He walked around us, smiling like this was a chat amongst friends and the four of us weren't his captives.

"Hello," he said. "My name is Radu. My apologies for the delay, I was detained elsewhere."

Unlike the rest of his men, Radu's accented English was perfect. Noted.

"There was some debate about what to do with you," he said, looking at each of us as he circled. "Four American students are more a liability than anything else. But then I was informed that three of you have very wealthy families."

My friends and I locked eyes with each other, nobody saying a word.

"Russell's information made me rethink my original plan of a shallow grave."

I glared at Russell. What an idiot. That was information we could have leveraged, but he had given it up for free.

Russell's gaze dropped to the table. "They were going to find out eventually."

I clenched my jaw and held my tongue. Getting into it with Russell over his mistake wouldn't help us now. I had to keep what was important at the forefront: staying alive.

This new knowledge changed things. *Adapt, Jess.*

Radu smiled. "Well, at least three of you are worth keeping alive for the time being."

A soldier stepped up behind Alena and yanked her head back by the hair, a blade already at her throat.

"So you're going to ransom us?" I asked, trying to direct attention away from Alena.

"Yes," Radu said. "I'm sure your families will pay well for your return."

"They will pay well for our return, *unharmed*. All four of us."

My heart kicked into high gear when Radu looked directly at me. I didn't dare look away or show weakness to this man, but that didn't mean that I wasn't terrified. His eyes narrowed, like he was evaluating me.

Then he nodded at the man who held Alena. She was out of the chair before I could move, and another man held me back from leaping after her. They threw her to the floor and began kicking her. I begged them to stop, other voices behind me as well, but all I could look at was my friend on the floor.

"That's enough." Radu's voice was quiet, but they heard it and stepped back. I was suddenly free, nearly collapsing next to Alena with my hands bound as they were, but I managed to turn her over. She was barely conscious, but still breathing.

"Take them back," he said.

I looked at him, memorizing his face and the conde-scending little smile that sat there. He'd pulled us out of the cells just to show us his power, and he'd used Alena to do it.

That he'd let us see his face made me nervous. Now I would never forget it, and he had to know that too.

He didn't plan to let us go, even if he sent ransom demands to our families. I needed to figure out how the hell to get us out of here.

I tried to take in everything again as they marched us back through the hallway, back toward the tiny cells.

Yes, three out of the four of us could be ransomed for quite a bit of money. But could it really have been sheer luck that they'd grabbed us specifically off the street?

This had to be tied to the stolen research.

I'd spent the past three months trying to figure out who'd been slowly siphoning out information from the Vandercroft biotechnology lab. There was only a small list of people who could have done it, and I'd been systematically crossing them off one by one.

The only two left I hadn't been able to confirm or eliminate were Russell and Susan. That had been the whole point of this vacation—to prompt some kind of action from them.

But being kidnapped was not the action I'd expected. I should have been more prepared, paid closer attention, expected something as grandiosely violent as a kidnapping.

But if this kidnapping was about the stolen research—and truly, it had to be—then Susan or Russell, or both, were far better actors than I'd given them credit for. Neither of them had given any sign whatsoever of knowing Radu or his men.

It couldn't be chance that we'd been picked up in Moldova. Nobody's luck was that bad.

I shouldn't have tried to handle this situation by myself. I should have told someone when I'd realized that there was a problem. The head of the fellowship program, or the London authorities. Or hell, one of the many, many former military men in my extended family who had spent their whole lives dealing with things like this.

At the very least, I should have told Ethan.

He had a way of looking at the world in a different light. He found things that I missed because he came at them from a different direction. Maybe if I had told him what I suspected— that someone was about to sell very dangerous biotechnological research findings to *bad guys*—he would have found the missing link, and none of us would be here.

The soldiers pushed us back into the cell. I managed to keep my feet, but Alena collapsed against the wall.

I hadn't told Alena about the research or that I'd suspected Russell or Susan. I'd wanted to be the hero. I'd made tracking their actions my primary goal.

Especially since Ethan had been so distant lately. He'd missed my birthday and then had seemed so much colder every time I'd talked to him since.

Damn it, I should've made him listen. Because poor Alena was the one who was suffering most.

The door closed behind us, and I went to her, thankful they hadn't chained me to the floor again. The rope still chafed at my wrists and was too tight to escape, but I could work with some movement. "Alena, talk to me. Are you okay?"

She groaned, but helped me a little when I got her to sit up. Blood dripped down her face, and she looked dazed. But her eyes were clear. That was something.

I brushed a strand of brown hair away from her face. "I'm so sorry."

She gave a tiny, weak laugh. "You in the habit of apologizing for crazy people now?"

"No, but it's my fault that we're here at all."

She shook her head, then winced, freezing. That had to hurt. "I think we all wanted to go on vacation."

"Only because I forced it." I needed to tell her the truth.

"What?"

At least she seemed a little more coherent now. Maybe this

was a good distraction from the pain. If I could keep her talking, that was good. "Someone's stealing research from the fellowship program. I'm positive it's Russell or Susan."

"How do you know?"

"That's why I've been sort of distracted lately. I've been following all their movements, hacking their emails and texts. I caught something about Moldova. I thought being here would do . . . something. Give me some intel to go on."

"Did it?"

"No." I leaned back against the stone wall. "The kidnapping was definitely unexpected. But I'm so sorry you've gotten so hurt."

Alena was so quiet that I thought that she'd passed out. Could her beating have caused internal bleeding? Severe damage? A spasm of fear gripped me for a moment, until she moved slowly and groaned.

Thank goodness. I wasn't happy she was in pain, but at least she was conscious. "Do you think the kidnappers are in on it? They didn't say anything about stolen research while I was with them. All they talked about was money."

I blew out a breath, fighting for a better hold on myself. I had to figure out what to do next. "I don't think so. But I can't be sure. I wish I knew what was happening with the others. Russell told him my and Susan's families had money. Did he offer them something else to get himself released? The research he stole?"

Alena slowly took a breath. "Let's focus on getting out of here. We can worry about stolen research later. I just want to go home."

"I know. Me too."

"But if they are looking for ransom, I don't have anyone who can pay. Not like you guys."

I slipped an arm around her. "You know that we have you

61

covered, Alena. My dad will pay for you, or someone in my family. I'm not going to leave you here with them. I promise."

Alena's eyes were closed, but she managed a small smile. "Thanks. But that doesn't mean we'll all make it, Jess. You know that. I have a horrible feeling about this."

So did I, but I didn't want to agree. I needed not to panic, to use my brain. It had never failed me before, and I would think of a way out of here now. Some way to negotiate with Radu and give him what he wanted, convince him it was in his best interest to let us all go unharmed.

The yell was the only warning we got before soldiers swarmed the cell. They had Alena up and on her feet in seconds, dragging her toward the door.

Oh God. "Stop!" I threw myself at one of them, knocking him off-balance.

Light flared behind my eyes as one of them struck me, and I went reeling, only to be caught by the rope binding my wrists. The soldier yanked me closer and slapped me across the face. Then again before someone else yelled at him. I was shoved back, and they all disappeared out the door before I could make a motion to stop them.

I had no breath left in my lungs. It had all been knocked out of me, and the left side of my face burned with pain. And that had been just a couple of slaps.

What would they do to Alena?

Panic clouded my focus. I had to do something to draw them back, to make them pay attention to me. I wasn't sure how much more Alena could take. As I forced myself to sit up, something was different. It took me a second to realize that the ropes on my hands were looser. They must have slipped when the guy grabbed them.

It wasn't much, but I didn't need much. One tiny mistake on their part would be enough.

I pulled up every memory I had about how to escape loosened bonds. There had been more than one lesson about that in the Linear Tactical classes. Twist my arms a certain way. Use my body for leverage.

It took far too long to get them loose, rubbing the skin raw on my wrists as I worked and twisted them. There was definitely blood on the ropes. But that worked in my favor, making the strands a little slicker. Just enough give for me to shove them off.

I wasn't expecting the pain that rushed through my arms in the absence of pressure, and I hissed out a breath. But it could be worse. Alena had gone through worse—was probably going through worse right now.

I had to help her. I could make them focus on me. Take out as many of them as I could. Get Alena out, get help, come back for Russell and Susan.

I couldn't see much in the dim light to work with in terms of weapons. The chains they had used to attach me to the floor were heavy, but bolted down and too far from the door. There was nothing else in here. Except . . .

There, in the corner. A piece of the wall was crumbling. Telltale signs of decay and little pebbles dotted the floor. When I pulled at the stone, it came away easily in chunks, and I kept going until I had one large enough to do some damage.

I was going to scream. Loud enough and long enough that one of them would have to come in here. They thought I was still bound, and they wouldn't see the rock coming.

Then I would get Alena out.

I was opening my mouth to scream when the door creaked open slowly. My heart rate spiked, and adrenaline surged through me. Every other time they'd come in, they'd clamored and slammed all around.

If this one was being quiet, he was here for something different.

JANE CROUCH

My skin crawled. One of Radu's men sneaking in here was not good.

I crouched, hiding as much as I could against the wall as the shape of a man crept forward. I would only have one shot at surprise. When he passed me, I leapt at him with my stone raised.

He whipped toward me, not caught a bit off guard, knocking the rock from my hand while wrapping an arm around my waist. I opened my mouth to scream, only to have a hand slap over it.

Then I really started to fight, but I couldn't get him away or get his hand off my mouth to scream. He was stronger than the rest, not throwing out punches just because he could. He was controlled and deadly.

I was in trouble.

CHAPTER NINE

Jess

I WASN'T GOING down like this. No matter what this guy had planned for me, I would fight.

He spun me around so my back was to him, keeping his hand over my mouth the whole time. Shit, he was strong. I squirmed and kicked, and it didn't make a difference in his hold on me.

"Stop fighting," the quiet voice said in ear. "I'm not here to hurt you."

All the fight drained out of me. Oh thank God. He was here, it was beyond every conceivable possibility, but he was here.

He still hadn't released my mouth. I reached up and touched his gloved hand.

"Don't scream." He released my mouth, and I turned, throwing myself against his chest.

"Ethan."

He froze. "Jess."

The word was no more than a breath, and his arms were

around me. Where they belonged. "Jess," he said again, lips in my hair.

I'd wished so hard that he was here, that I could be with him, that it felt like I'd conjured him out of thin air. I wanted to kiss him and remain like this, locked in his arms for the rest of forever. But we didn't have time for that. Forever would have to wait.

"How did you find me?" I kept my voice to a whisper.

Ethan hesitated before speaking, never once letting me go. "The government brought me in."

I gasped. "They sent a SEAL team for us?"

In the pale light from the door, I saw him wince. "Not exactly. It's a team of four." There was black paint smudged on his face to match his dark clothing, but it didn't disguise how handsome he was—his strong jaw, carved cheeks.

Ethan had always been beautiful. But never more than now when he was an avenging angel come to save me.

But a team of four? That was strange. It wasn't close to a full team. What did that mean? I would have to ask more later.

"We need to find Alena," I said. "They just took her."

He nodded. "Let's go."

Unlike before, this time when we entered the hallway, it was empty. Were the number of soldiers that I'd seen just a show of force? Where were they?

Voices sounded to the right, and Ethan pulled me behind him as he crept down the hallway toward the only visible door. He had a gun in his hand down by his side. Holding out his other hand, he motioned me back. I hesitated, unsure what he had planned, but I wanted to get in there. I could hear them laughing.

Without warning, Ethan kicked open the door. One powerful blow. A shout followed, and I stayed behind him as he swept into the room firing off three shots in rapid succession. Tranquilizer darts found their targets in the necks and chests of three soldiers. The last one was too close to get a shot off, and I yelled my warning too late.

The man jumped on Ethan, and they went down together. But Ethan wasn't fazed. He flipped the man onto his back, delivering two sharp blows to the man's jaw, stunning him. He retrieved his gun and shot him with one of the tranquilizers to complete the takedown.

Holy shit. I knew that Ethan was a SEAL and that he'd gone through all the SEAL BUD/s training. But he'd told me he was a field medic. He'd made it seem like nothing. Boring. Easy.

He hadn't told me he could turn into a kick-ass action hero on demand. And it was sexy as hell.

But we needed to find Alena. I didn't see her.

"I have to find my friend Alena. They've been hardest on her."

Ethan watched the door, holding the dart gun ready. Nonlethal force. But I spied the real gun on his hip. He would do what he needed to, if it came to it.

The slightest sniffle caught my ears, and I pushed open a curtain to find a back room. Alena was sitting on a couch, staring at nothing. Her clothes looked intact, but it had taken me so long to get out of the ropes that anything could have happened. Had she been traumatized? Assaulted?

"Alena." I crouched next to her.

Her eyes snapped to me like she hadn't noticed me— retreated so deep inside that there was nothing left. As soon as she saw me, she burst into tears. "Jess."

I held her close while she sobbed, unsure what to do. I wanted to cry with her.

A gentle hand touched my shoulder. Ethan looked down at me. His face wasn't unsympathetic, but it was also firm. Ready. I knew that look. I'd seen it on the faces of the Linear Tactical men my entire life.

Ethan was in mission mode, and we were still in danger. Falling apart would have to wait. Survival first.

"We need to be as quiet as we can," he whispered, "and we need to move. The rest of my team is getting your other two friends out. There's a place we're supposed to meet."

He crouched down in front of Alena, eyes running over her quickly, assessing. "Can you walk, Alena?"

She was still crying, but she nodded.

"Okay. I'm going to make sure the way is clear, and then we need to go."

Our eyes met for a moment, and something passed between us, though it was hard to say what. There was too much that had gone unsaid for too long. But he was here, and that was all that mattered.

~

ETHAN

JESS WAS ALIVE AND UNHURT.

Alive and unhurt.

That thought kept running through my mind as I checked the hallway to make sure that it was still clear.

There were bruises on her face that made me contemplate switching to real bullets, but she was moving well, and she'd suffered far less than her friend.

The relief I'd felt when I'd pulled her into my arms wasn't something I was going to forget anytime in the next one hundred years or so. It had been so sharp, so acute, that I felt like a changed person.

I felt whole. Because the other half of me was back where it belonged.

She was so fucking beautiful, even covered in dirt and

anger, and I knew that I would never let anything come between us again. Forget formulating a plan and wooing her.

I wasn't leaving her side unless she asked me to let her go. And even then, I would still love her.

That was what beat in my chest. True, pure love. There had never been, and there never would be, anyone else. I just had to get her the hell out of here and tell her that.

I ducked back into the room, running my eyes over the fallen combatants. No signs of movement. There shouldn't be —the tranq we used was powerful enough to put down an elephant—but I wasn't about to take chances because a dart hadn't connected properly. Behind the curtain, it was quieter. Jess had Alena on her feet, arm wrapped around the girl who was still silently crying. But at least she was ready to move.

I would get her somewhere safe enough to cry properly.

"Ready?"

Jess nodded. The determination in her eyes was enough to make me fall in love with her all over again. She hadn't given up. Not for a second. Hell, she'd almost taken me down with that rock in the cell, and I was damn proud of her that she'd been willing to try.

They stuck close behind me as I led the way. We were going out the way that I'd come in. So far, everything had gone like clockwork. The only thing left was to get to the vehicles and get out.

Alena was limping, but we moved at a decent pace. Not one of the guards had moved from where I had dropped them. The back door was still free, and I couldn't hear any other signs of movement in the building—which was exactly how it should be if the others were doing their jobs.

There would have to be a slight change in plan since Alena couldn't descend the rocks with any kind of leg injury. The path to the west should be clear. I looked both directions out of the building before gesturing them forward. "Stay close to me."

We clung to the shadows as we moved around the building until I saw a silhouette against the dark sky. I snapped my fingers twice and got three in return. "Landon," I said.

"Ethan."

"Got them."

He nodded. "Edge of the woods, then hold. Go."

We moved as one quickly down the hill. I pushed Jess and Alena in front of me so I could cover them from behind. Though I didn't see any shapes on the rooftops, that could change at any second if we'd missed someone.

As soon as we reached the tree line, I pulled them to a stop, and we crouched low in the shadows, waiting. Not five minutes later, four figures ran down the hill and met us. Russell and Susan looked all right from what I could see. No one injured enough to need carrying, which had been our biggest fear.

Landon leaned in. "I'm scouting ahead for confirmation. Move as quietly as possible until we reach the vehicles."

He disappeared into the woods like smoke on the wind, and that one movement told me more about his skills than anything else. The man was lethal, and he wouldn't let anything stop him. Isaac motioned us forward when we'd let him have enough of a head start. He led through the woods, and I trailed behind, MacQueen covering the center.

It was slow moving, being as quiet as we were, and the civilians were louder than we could afford, but they were doing their best. The distance to the vehicles was only a mile, but it felt like five at the pace we were moving.

We had almost reached the clearing when I heard the sound.

Two snaps.

The other team members froze with me while Jess and the others followed suit, suddenly sensing our tension. Landon materialized, and I stepped up at his hurried whisper. "We've been made somehow. The woods beyond the vehicles are filled with patrols. We won't get a hundred meters."

Isaac cursed under his breath. "Who tipped them off?"

"Maybe we were spotted coming in," MacQueen said.

It didn't seem likely, but we couldn't rule it out either. Either way, there was no way an ambush waited just beyond our vehicles by chance.

Could MacQueen have tipped them off? Russell? Susan?

"We head for the town on foot," Isaac said. "Get close and hide before the sun rises. Secure new vehicles to get the hell out of here."

Eight people were conspicuous under the best of circumstances, and these were far from that.

"Ethan, take point while I go up ahead," Landon said. "Isaac, you're the rear."

I heard what he wasn't saying: he wanted Isaac at the back of the group to watch MacQueen now that we knew someone had tipped off the enemy. We'd have to make sure we knew every move that he made.

Had he really been going to the bathroom on the plane? Or had he been making a well-timed phone call?

Landon disappeared after I nodded. By now I had hoped to be driving away, well on our way out so I could get Jess somewhere safe and talk to her.

Wasn't going to happen as soon as I'd hoped.

We moved to the east, cutting back through the woods and away from the line of soldiers. Thankfully, they were far enough away that we could afford a little more noise. I glanced back when I heard whispers and had to lock my jaw in place to tamp down the spike of jealousy rocking me.

Russell Kramer was next to Jess. Far closer than was strictly necessary for walking through the woods. He asked her if she was hurt and briefly recapped what he'd gone through at the hands of the kidnappers.

All I could see was her birthday party. Walking into the bar and finding them just as close as they were now, his eyes all over her as if he had the right.

Not that I blamed him for wanting to be close to Jess. That didn't mean I wasn't about to knock his teeth out.

Russell started telling a sob story about how one of the bad guys had punched him in the gut a couple of times. Maybe Jess could look at it when they stopped and make sure the bruising wasn't too bad.

You know what? Maybe we needed some quiet after all.

"Think you both could save the sweet nothings for when we're no longer in danger?"

Jess's eyes snapped to mine, hurt obvious even in the shadows. Fuck. My tone had been harsher than I'd intended, though it had the desired effect of getting Russell to back the hell off.

But I hated that look on Jess's face. She'd just been through hell, and I was acting like an ass.

I reached for her out of instinct. "I'm sorry. We just . . . need to keep chatter to a minimum if possible."

Jess stepped toward me, only a breath away, about to say something. I wanted to kiss her more than I wanted my next breath. I should've done it the second I found her in that room.

"Hey man, exactly where are we going?"

I glared at Russell for the interruption. But we needed to get going. The personal stuff with Jess would have to wait.

I tilted my head to the side. "This way."

My sole focus needed to be on the mission. Everything else would have to wait.

CHAPTER TEN

THREE YEARS Ago
  Ethan - 21
  Jess - 18

JESS HAD BEEN eighteen for five minutes.

For her birthday, her mom and dad had offered to take her anywhere she wanted to go. On a trip, or home to Oak Creek. As much as she loved her parents and her sister, there was only one place she wanted to be as she turned eighteen.

Wherever Ethan Bollinger was.

Of course, that was true for any birthday, but it was especially true for this one. She was finally an adult. Mentally and emotionally, she'd been an adult for a lot longer than five minutes, but *legally* she was now eighteen.

Legally was the only thing she cared about because Ethan was now out of excuses for not giving her what she wanted: *him.*

She'd asked for him for her past two birthdays, but he was having none of it. Protecting her from herself, he called it. Told her they had all the time in the world to have sex with each other. He could wait until she was legally an adult.

With anyone else, she probably would have thought he was just covering his own ass, but not Ethan. So protective. Such a gentleman. It was part of the reason she loved him so much.

He was on leave from his SEAL team for a couple of days, and since his team was stationed in Germany, she and Ethan were meeting in Paris. Short flights for both of them.

When her parents had found out this was where she was going, they'd offered to take her dad's jet and meet her here. She'd hemmed and hawed, and tried to make excuses for them not to come, but knew they were going to show up anyway. Finally, she'd told her mom she was meeting Ethan here and that they should very definitely not come.

She'd left poor Mom to explain things to Dad and hoped he didn't show up with a shotgun. That would not be the romantic weekend she had planned. Her mom had been a little impressed that they had waited this long.

That was testimony of Ethan's willpower, because God knew Jess had been trying to talk him into more for forever. Literally every time they'd seen each other for the past year and a half, she'd tried to seduce him.

And while he would kiss her all day long, he'd never do any more than that.

Well, occasionally more than that.

He'd never stopped her from rubbing up against him, and not even his infamous willpower could withstand her climbing on top of him when they kissed. Which is why he always made sure they remained dressed.

So she knew he wanted her, but he'd never let her do anything to him—touch him the way she wanted to with her hands and her mouth. She may only be eighteen, but she had a mind that allowed her to think of unlimited situations and scenarios with the two of them.

She and Ethan were supposed to meet tomorrow, or technically later today, for her birthday, but she'd arrived early. And thanks to a little bit of hacking that Uncle Kendrick and Aunt Neo had taught her, she knew that Ethan had arrived a day early too.

She was sure he had some big, romantic day planned for them tomorrow. Maybe dinner at the restaurant on the Eiffel Tower, or a tour of the Louvre, and she wanted to do all that with him. She wanted to do everything this world had to offer with her Ethan.

But right now, she just wanted *him*.

It was after midnight, and he might be asleep. She didn't care. She got off the elevator and walked down the hall toward his room. She had a trench coat on with only a matching bra and panty set underneath. She was like some bad 1980s movie hooker, but she didn't care. She didn't want to waste time having to pull off pants and shirts. She'd wasted enough time waiting for this.

She had half a dozen condoms in the coat pocket, but she'd also been on the pill for more than a year. She hoped she could talk him into *not* using the condoms.

But the only thing that gave her the slightest moment of hesitation was that he'd been legal for quite a bit longer than she had.

He'd been in the Navy now for four years, had been a Navy SEAL for three of those years, one of the youngest people to ever complete SEAL training. She couldn't hide from the fact that it was possible, maybe even probable, that he'd had sex with someone else at some point.

Her heart cracked at the thought of it. The image of his lips kissing another woman, his body close to hers, made Jess want to go rip some bimbo's hair out. But she refused to allow that to come between them now.

It was her own fault. She'd written him that letter after

he'd joined the Navy telling him he could do what he wanted. She hadn't wanted him to feel trapped, and although she'd never so much as looked at another boy, not that there were that many appealing choices at Vandercroft, she hadn't wanted to keep Ethan from doing what he really wanted. Even if that was sexual relations with another woman.

But that clause was over now. She was eighteen, a woman, and he was her man. Hers alone.

She arrived in front of his door and tapped on it. She stood there, hands on her hips, knowing he would look through the security hole before opening the door.

And then there he was.

Her eyes drank in the sight of him. It had been six months since she'd last seen him face-to-face. His dark hair was a little longer than someone would expect a Navy SEAL's to be, and he had a slight beard. She knew what that meant. He'd been doing undercover missions where a cropped haircut and a clean-shaven face would be out of place.

His hair was tussled now, and a little damp. He'd gotten out of the shower recently. Opted to go without a shirt. Thank the Lord.

It was all she could do not to reach up and run her nails down over his pecs and across those abs. She knew enough about biology to have known years ago that Ethan was going to resemble his father in terms of physique: tall, muscular. But Ethan was a specimen unto himself. And right for *her*. She forced her gaze away from that torso and back up to his green eyes. Her Ethan's eyes.

"Hi," she said.

He leaned against the doorframe. "I thought we were meeting tomorrow."

"I got here early."

He raised one dark eyebrow. "And don't tell me, you hacked

the hotel's computer system and figured out I was here early too?"

He knew her way too well. *"Moi?"* she asked, appropriate since they were in Paris.

Just when she'd thought she would have to ask for an invite in, he reached out and hooked a hand behind her neck and dragged her against him.

His lips crashed into hers, fitting perfectly the way they had since their first kiss.

"I missed you." They both said it at the same time against each other's mouths.

She slid her arms around his waist and pulled him closer. "I couldn't wait until tomorrow to see you, knowing that you were here tonight."

"I'm glad." He closed the door behind them as they backed farther into the hotel room. "I thought you were somewhere nearby. I can always feel it when you're nearby, but I thought maybe that was just wishful thinking on my part. I'm glad to have every extra second with you I can get."

They both always felt that way. Both looked forward to a time in the future when they wouldn't have to be apart and spend stolen minutes together.

His lips left hers. "Do you want to take off your coat?"

She couldn't stop the smile that took over her face. She'd been wanting to do this for a very long time. "Yes."

He reached for the belt to help her, but she stepped back so she could do it herself. "Allow me."

Academically, she'd always wondered if she would be shy when this moment came, even though shyness wasn't a natural state for her. She'd wondered if she would be nervous when it was time to make love with Ethan for the first time.

She wasn't. She unhooked the belt and slid the coat off her shoulder, although not letting it slide to the floor. Ethan's breath hissed through his teeth, increasing her confidence.

But then he stepped back a little.

"Sweet God, Jess."

"Do you like?"

"Do I like? Did you wander around the hotel in that outfit?"

"Oh, come on." She rolled her eyes. The undergarments weren't *that* risqué. "You've seen me in less than this, in a bathing suit at Pike's Peak every summer since we've known each other."

Now she was starting to feel a little bit insecure.

"I . . ." Ethan swallowed loudly. "I . . ."

He was staring down at her. Green eyes moving down her body, then back up.

This wasn't about him not wanting her. She'd caught him off guard, and he needed a moment to adjust. She knew him well enough to know that.

Ethan wasn't smart like her. He was smart in an entirely different way. He was calm under pressure, able to focus where she sometimes tended to panic, when her brain tried to work through too many scenarios at once.

Ethan focused on one, sorting through it before moving on to the next.

"You know why I'm here, E," she said, "I'm eighteen."

He folded his arms over his chest. "You've been eighteen for thirty seconds."

"Twelve and a half minutes," she muttered before stepping closer. "I know what I want. I want you."

He scrubbed a hand over his face. "It doesn't have to be tonight, Jess. It doesn't have to be this weekend. We have forever."

She pulled the coat back around her body. "Is this not what you want?"

"That's not what I'm saying. But it's most important to me that you know we don't have any sort of timetable. Just because you're legal doesn't mean we have to fall into bed."

She waved her arm around the lovely hotel room with a big king bed sitting in the middle of it. "We're meeting in Paris. We're in a hotel room. I thought all of that was leading to us finally making love together."

He walked a little further into the room and opened the door at that wall. "I got us connecting rooms. I didn't want you to feel pressured."

She let out a sigh. Of course he had gotten two rooms.

As if Ethan could ever make her feel pressured. As if she didn't want him more than she wanted her next breath. She walked over to him, reaching up to cup his cheeks.

"You are a good man, and you have always taken care of me. We will have a wonderful time this weekend, and it can be with or without sex. But I just have one question I want you to answer first."

"Anything." His hands fell to her waist as if he couldn't help himself.

"Do you want me?"

He immediately opened his mouth, but she stopped him with a finger on his lips. "I know you love me, Ethan, but our relationship is different than most people's. We've known each other for so long. We've grown up together. If what you feel for me is not sexual in nature, now is the time for you to tell me."

She honestly didn't know what she was going to do if he told her that the love he felt for her had turned platonic at some point. She loved him platonically, but she also loved him every other way that a person could love another, and that very definitely included sexually.

She loved him enough to let him go if that was what he needed. Even though it might rip her heart out.

He didn't say anything, just stepped closer, and her heart caught in her throat. Maybe things really had changed for him. He trailed gentle fingers down her cheek, and she found herself blinking back tears.

But his hands kept moving, brushing down her neck, then under the collar of her coat before sliding it off her shoulders.

The coat fell to the ground behind her. His fingers didn't stop. They traced down her back before unhooking her bra and pulling it away from her body. It joined the coat on the ground.

He dropped down to one knee and then the other, his lips kissing along her belly as he hooked his fingers into the strappy elastic at the waist of her underwear and slid that down also. As he kissed along her belly again, her fingers found their way into his hair.

He glanced up at her. "I've been waiting for this moment my entire adult life. If you had told me you needed more time this weekend, I would have somehow found the strength to give it to you, but do not doubt that I want you. Never doubt that."

ETHAN HAD SEEN many looks in Jess's eyes over the years. He'd seen them blaze with anger, with protectiveness, with compassion.

But seeing them fill with tears of insecurity because she'd thought he wasn't interested in making love to her was not something he ever wanted to see again.

He'd been telling her nothing less than the truth when he'd said he would have found the strength to ease back if she'd needed the distance this weekend. He would have done it, of course, because there was nothing he wouldn't do for the woman now standing naked in front of him.

And she was a woman. In every way that someone could be a woman.

And she was *his*.

"I love you, Jess," he whispered as he peppered kisses along the smooth skin of her hips. "I want you. I consider myself the luckiest man on the planet because you came here tonight rather than waiting until tomorrow."

He made his way back up her body, spending ample time on her gorgeous breasts, trying to keep himself under control.

When he was finally back at her lips, he cupped her cheeks so she was looking directly into his eyes. "I want you. We're never going to get another first time, so I want to do this slow, and I want to make it right for both of us. But don't doubt I want you."

"Is it your first time too? It's okay if it's not. I know we agreed that it was okay for us to see other people. I didn't, but if you did, I understand."

"Jessica Elizabeth O'Conner." He shook his head. "There has never been anyone else for me but you. I didn't care how much permission you'd given me. If you had dropped off a naked woman in my room and told me to go at it, I still wouldn't have cared. If it's not you, I'm not interested. You're the only person I'll ever have sex with, you're the only person I'll ever kiss, and you're the only woman I'll ever love."

Her face lit up, and then a devious smile turned her lips up. There she was. There was his little genius.

"If it's the first time for both of us, then we're going to have to do a *lot* of experimenting to get it right."

She reached down, hooked her hands into his sweat pants, and pulled them down over his hips. He used his leg to hook them and pull them the rest of the way off. And then, for the first time ever, they were both naked together.

She kissed her way across his chest, and he pushed up against her in a way that made it very obvious that he definitely wanted her.

She nipped him on his chest, and he grabbed her hips with a groan, sliding his hands under her thighs and lifting her up so he could trap her between the wall and his body. Both of them let out a gasp.

"We're definitely going to need a lot of experimenting," he said before his lips found hers once more.

She hiked her legs around his waist, and he walked them over to the bed and lowered her.

"I have condoms," she said. "But I'm also on the pill, so I'm okay with not using them if you are."

He could barely stop staring down at her naked body long enough to process what she was saying. But he nodded. Having nothing between them when he was inside her? He couldn't imagine anything better on this earth.

It was one of the rewards for both of them having waited. Having never been with anyone else but each other. That wait hadn't always been easy, so he would gladly enjoy these spoils.

"You're so beautiful, Jess. I mean, I've always known you were, but . . . you take my breath away."

She opened her arms up to him with a smile. "Thank you for waiting for me. I know I didn't always make it easy, but I promise, you and I together will be worth the wait."

He had no doubt. It would start great today and only get better for the rest of their lives.

CHAPTER ELEVEN

ETHAN

ONE OF THE few good things about being in the middle of nowhere in a moderately undeveloped country was the fact that there were a fair number of abandoned buildings to hide in, like the barn we currently occupied.

It was falling apart, and wouldn't make good shelter if the weather turned nasty, but it was good enough to keep us out of sight during the daylight hours. It was midafternoon, verging on evening. Isaac would be leaving soon to go scouting. Landon had just gotten back.

I didn't like that we were only half a mile from the small town. Too many opportunities to be accidentally spotted. But it was also our best bet for finding some transportation and getting out of here quickly. The backup evacuation site was nearly twenty miles away.

Landon sat up against the wall of the barn, resting after his turn out surveilling.

"It's not good," he said quietly. "Radu's soldiers are everywhere, going door to door. Getting around them to the backup site isn't going to be easy."

Radu wasn't giving up, and I wasn't surprised. If he was hoping to ransom three people to wealthy families, that would be a huge amount of money—well worth trying to find them. And if he was the contact for buying the stolen research, that was even more reason to hunt down Jess and her friends.

But if it was Russell or Susan, why hadn't they given the research to Radu already?

Isaac crossed his arms over his chest. "We need to split up."

I scrubbed a hand down my face. He was right, but I didn't like it. "I agree but it complicates things."

A group of eight, especially with four civilians, one wounded, was basically a fucking circus and drew so much attention. Impossible to keep covert. Splitting up was the only viable option.

But splitting up also meant dividing our manpower, weapons, and resources.

"What's the car situation?" Isaac asked Landon.

"There are some, but in a town this size most stolen vehicles are going to be quickly noticed."

Isaac nodded. He was about to leave for recon. "Okay. I'll see what I can find."

We needed a vehicle. Twenty miles was a long way, especially for Alena and the beating she'd taken. Jess would make it. Susan and Russell . . . I hadn't gotten a good reading on their mental and physical fortitude yet.

"I'll take outside lookout for a while," Landon said. "You and MacQueen stay here. Take turns on watch from the south."

I heard the unspoken implication: watch MacQueen while they couldn't. I nodded.

Landon turned to everyone else. "You guys rest. We're going to move once it gets dark, so conserve as much energy as you can. Eat and drink." They'd already handed out the calorie-dense nutrition bars they'd brought. They'd found a stream on the way toward town and filled up their water bottles using purifying tablets to make sure it was drinkable.

Landon and Isaac both disappeared out of the front of the barn. Landon would be hidden, watching for anyone coming our direction from the town, and MacQueen and I would take turns watching out the back. MacQueen didn't say anything as he crossed the space to take up the post, claiming the first stretch. That was fine with me.

I moved to an empty corner and sat. From here, I had a good vantage of the entire space, and the shadows allowed me the most privacy that I was going to get right now. Of course, my eyes immediately went to Jess, and I wished that they hadn't.

Russell was once again far too close to her, trying to help her clean the deep scrapes on her wrists she'd gotten escaping her restraints. The fact that she'd been able to do that made me damn proud. But the wounds still needed attention.

Russell was attempting to use the wipes and bandages from the first aid kit we'd brought to tend to Jess's wrists. Coddling her. Being too gentle. The guy couldn't see her growing annoyance with being treated like she was fragile.

I covered my mouth with my hand to hide my smile. Even from across the room, Jess's frustration with him was obvious. Her shoulders were tense and lips were tight. Jess liked to do things herself—even when it wasn't the easiest way—because her brain liked as much information as possible. She learned better by doing.

But Russell hadn't learned that, and the way he was currently babying her was getting on her nerves. He probably thought that was what women wanted and liked. And maybe most women would, but not Jess. Not *my* woman.

I snorted when she gently but firmly pulled Russell's hand away from her arm and put it in his lap, quickly finishing wrapping her own wrists and putting everything back in the kit.

The smile she gave him looked real, and to anyone who didn't know her, they'd probably be dazzled. But it wasn't her real smile. I knew her real smile intimately, and this wasn't it. She got up and moved to the other side of the barn to sit with Alena and Susan. Refuge.

I smothered a laugh at the look on Russell's face—that bemused, hopeful expression. He had no idea how hard he'd just been rejected.

That laugh died in my chest when Russell looked at me, then headed over. I got it. He didn't want to sit there alone.

There was no part of me interested in chatting with Russell Kramer. I knew I could get up and make an excuse that I had to keep watch to get out of it. But my gut told me not to do that.

Right now was an opportunity to do what I did best. Listen. Observe. Analyze. Maybe I'd get some insight as to whether Russell was the one who'd stolen the research.

Maybe I'd get some insight into the man who was trying to make moves on the woman I'd been in love with for more than fifteen years.

Russell sat down beside me with a sigh. I wasn't going to speak first. One of the things I'd learned early was that silence made people want to talk. If you kept quiet, everyone around you wanted to fill the space with words, to the point that they didn't always realize what they were saying.

"So you're Jess's cousin, right?"

That wasn't what I'd expected him to fill the silence with. "Excuse me?"

"Jess mentioned that she had a cousin in the SEALs. Or . . . she said her aunt and uncle's kid. That's a cousin, right?"

"Right," I said without elaborating.

Jess did consider my parents her aunt and uncle. Everyone in our extended Linear Tactical family circle were aunts and uncles. But apparently, Jess hadn't corrected Russell on his assumption that she and I were related. So even though it burned me alive, I didn't correct him either.

Her *cousin*?

In the SEALs, my code name had been Saint. Partly because I wasn't a partier, and I usually ended up as the designated driver whenever the guys wanted to have a night where they got a little out of hand. And because, unlike my fellow sailors, I never used my SEAL status to score women. I wasn't interested in anyone who wasn't Jess.

But they'd also given me the code name because I didn't lose my cool. I stayed focused and calm despite whatever was thrown at me. It was that focus and determination my superiors had seen, allowing me to start and complete BUD/S when I was still a teenager—something nearly unheard of—and why they'd sent me on to become a field medic.

But being called Jess's fucking *cousin*? I could kill Russell Kramer right now in about a dozen ways with my bare hands, and no one in the room would even notice until it was too late. And fuck, I was tempted.

Her *cousin*. The word burned in my chest, anger and jealousy filling me with sharp energy that I had to shove down to keep contained.

"How do you know Jess?" I asked, hiding the effort it took to keep my voice even.

"Oh, we're in the same fellowship program in London. The Vandercroft Biotechnology Fellowship. Jess has been there a lot longer than I have. But I've been there for about two years now. Honestly, we didn't know each other that well until six months ago. We're on the same team now."

I took a breath in and let it out. "So you work closely together?"

"Yeah," Russell said with a laugh. "But I think that basking in Jess's greatness would be more accurate. She's pretty amazing, though sometimes hard to read."

I grit my teeth. "Yeah?"

"I was interested in her right away—who wouldn't be, right? But I don't think she knew I existed until around her birthday a couple months ago. And then, bam, she's flirting with me like crazy. I couldn't believe it."

I felt like I was choking on my own voice. "Yeah? You and my *cuz* dating now?"

If he said yes, I wouldn't fall apart. I would handle it. It was always in the back of my mind that this could happen.

Because of her mind and her intellect, Jess needed to push her boundaries in every way. The same could go for dating. And as much as I hated to admit it, just because I'd never had the desire to so much as look at another woman, it didn't mean things were the same for Jess.

If Jess was going to be mine, it had to be because she *wanted* it. Not because it was the default setting she'd known her whole life.

That didn't mean I didn't want to let out a roar right now and tear this entire structure down.

But everything in me released when Russell shook his head. "No, we're not dating. She's actually kind of . . . strange?" He scratched the back of his head like he was trying to solve a puzzle. "I don't know. Maybe it's because she's been at the project since she was really young. I'm not sure she knows how to act around men."

"Yeah?" Thank God this dude was willing to spill his guts to a complete stranger.

"Could have sworn that she was interested. But it only ever goes up to a certain point. If I get too close, make any sort of real move, she completely shuts me down." He turned to me. "Is this weird me saying this to you, since you guys are family?"

Jess was my family, that much was true. "No, it's fine. Continue."

Russell shrugged. "She's never even let me kiss her, let alone anything else that I might have wanted. Sorry man, that has to be weird for you."

No, not weird. What it was, was sweet, cool relief. Russell had never touched her, and Jess had never asked him to.

Like she'd heard me call her name in her thoughts, Jess looked over and met my eyes. No doubt she wanted to know what Russell and I were talking about.

It wasn't long before Isaac reentered the barn, followed quickly by Landon. He had a bag with him and dropped it on the floor in the middle of the room. "More food. Water."

I hadn't eaten anything all day but let the civilians get to the fresh food first. They were burning more calories than us, thanks to fluctuating cortisol levels from stress and fear.

Jess hung back too, letting her friends eat first before grabbing some fruit. I stepped to the side to listen to Isaac's report, still keeping an eye on everyone else.

"I found a vehicle out in one farm's field that might not be noticed for a while," Isaac said. "But it can only fit five."

Not ideal. "So we split five and three?"

Landon nodded. "A group of three would be easier to conceal. Get to the next town and steal a vehicle there so we're less conspicuous."

The next town was five miles down the road. Doable, at the very least.

"How are we going to split?" MacQueen asked.

Landon glanced at me, then Isaac. "Ethan can go with the four civilians."

"No," MacQueen responded instantly. "I'm not leaving Russell. I'll take them."

There was no way in hell I was going to let that happen. "Fuck that, I'm not leaving Jess."

I would leave her with Isaac or Landon but I definitely wasn't leaving her with MacQueen.

Isaac held a hand up. "Ethan, you'll take two of the civvies and get to the next town to steal the vehicle. The rest of us will take the car." He looked at me hard, and it wasn't difficult to make the leap.

Two noncivilians needed to be with MacQueen in case he was in on this. Landon and Isaac had worked together long enough to know how to communicate silently. They were the logical choice to watch MacQueen together.

I didn't mind stealing a second vehicle in the next town. Five miles wasn't far. "Understood."

MacQueen didn't argue either.

"All right," Isaac called quietly, but loud enough for everyone in the barn to hear him. "Bunk down and get some rest. We're moving in a few hours once it gets dark and the town settles down, and you'll need all your energy."

I nodded to MacQueen. "I'll take watch."

We traded places at the back of the barn, and I scanned the tree-covered horizon. Nothing suspicious. For now. Behind me were the quiet sounds of people trying to get comfortable when there was little comfort to be had.

One shuffle was a little louder, and I glanced back to find Jess near me. I didn't move, since it was clear she was trying not to draw any attention, and she didn't stand until she was close.

And she was close. Standing so near that I could feel her heat on my skin. I itched to touch her, but I folded my arms instead. There was too much between us to skip right to where I so desperately wanted to be.

I managed a smile since I could feel her gaze on me. "Hey, cuz. Is that what I should call you now?"

I took my eyes off the horizon for a second and found her blushing. "It's not what you think, Ethan. I promise."

I sighed. "You sure about that?"

"Yes. Russell is—"

"I came to London for your birthday," I said quietly, cutting her off. "I got leave and came to surprise you."

"What?" Shock laced her voice.

"Yep. Got there just in time to see you fawning all over Russell. Dancing." I nodded over my shoulder in Russell's directions. "You looked . . . cozy."

"It's not what you think," she said again.

"I know we have a lot to talk about, but I just need to know one thing."

"Yeah?"

I turned toward her. "We're splitting up."

"What?" Her voice dripped with panic. "No. No, I don't want that. Please. I'm sorry. I—"

Shit. She thought I meant the two of *us* splitting up. Not the mission. "Jess, I mean when we leave here. The group has to split up because we can't all fit in one car."

"Oh."

"Two of you will go with Isaac, Landon, and MacQueen. Russell is one of those. The other two will come with me. So you have to choose. Do you want to go with Russell? Or stay with me?"

A moment passed, and Jess's jaw dropped. Her voice was a shocked gasp. "I can't believe you have to ask me that."

I couldn't believe I had to either. Before two months ago, the thought would never have crossed my mind. I would have been sure of her answer.

Now I wasn't, despite Russell's overshare that they hadn't so much as kissed. But I didn't say any of that out loud, because I still needed her answer.

"I want to go with you," she said. "Always you."

I nodded. "Okay."

"But . . ." she said. "We do need to talk, Ethan. There are things that you don't know."

Before I could respond—not that I knew how to respond to that—she went back to her spot by Alena and lay down, curling onto her side and doing her best to get comfortable.

There were things I didn't know. That's exactly what I was afraid of. With Jess, I'd always known everything. We'd been sure.

Not knowing where we stood felt like being without an anchor in a storm. It wouldn't take much to lose my footing and drown.

I took one last look at her on the ground, wishing I could hold her. Holding Jess was a constant I was familiar with, and I ached for it.

How the hell had we gotten to the place where I couldn't?

CHAPTER TWELVE

Jess

I COULDN'T SLEEP. God knew my body was tired, but my thoughts were moving so quickly it seemed impossible to relax enough to even close my eyes.

Everything had gotten worse, and, once again, it was my fault. I hadn't thought it could get any worse, but obviously I'd been wrong. Not only were we running for our lives, but Ethan and I were barely speaking. The tension between us was awkward and strange, and I hated it. That was my fault too.

He had been there. On my birthday. Had seen *everything*.

Vivid flashes of that night kept playing in my mind. Me flirting with Russell and laughing at his jokes. Hugging him and dancing with him more than I really wanted to. It was all a lie, but Ethan didn't know that.

I covered my face with my hands even though it was dark and no one was looking at me anyway. My skin was hot with a furious blush. What did he think of me? I'd told him the situation wasn't what he thought, but I had no idea what that was. It had to be the worst.

No wonder things had been strained and distant between us the past couple of months. I'd been all pissy and holier-than-thou because I thought he'd forgotten my birthday. I'd been such a brat to him, expecting an apology.

But he'd been distant because he'd thought I wanted to be with someone else. With Russell. The thought brought tears to my eyes. I couldn't stand to think I'd hurt Ethan.

And the thought that our relationship might be over . . . it ripped a gaping hole in my chest.

I needed to tell him everything as soon as humanly possible. This was far beyond the point of me solving it by myself. Me and my stupid pride shouldn't have tried to do it to begin with.

Tell Ethan, get out of this awful situation alive, and then get back to London and talk to the program heads. Show them what I'd been doing for the past few months and let them know I was certain it was either Russell or Susan who'd been planning to sell stolen secrets, but that I didn't know which.

And then confess that I'd actually stolen the research myself.

I scrubbed my hands down my face. This had to be handled delicately because ultimately I was the one who'd taken the real data—biotech research that could easily be weaponized—without permission. I could very easily be portrayed as the bad guy if things went wrong.

But whoever had been siphoning info had been siphoning *false* info. I'd taken the real data and left carefully curated but utterly false information in its place. No one would be able to tell the difference at a glance.

The most important thing right now was keeping the real research safe. I hadn't taken any chances, keeping it on me at all times. The microchip wasn't hard to hide in the locket that I always wore—a gift from Ethan.

So if someone tried to sell what they'd stolen, they were in for an unpleasant surprise.

What I was most worried about right now was my relationship with Ethan. He had always been the most important thing in my life. And still was. More than any of the work I'd done over the years.

And it killed me that I'd put that relationship in danger, even if I'd done it for a good reason.

Sleep wasn't going to happen, so I settled for rest instead. I tried to relax as much as I could as darkness fell around us. Alena, Russell, and Susan all fell asleep, and it wasn't long before it was time to go.

We were shaken awake and told to gather whatever things we had. It was Ethan who reached for me, and I grabbed his hand before he could move away.

The contact was electric. Like it always had been. Even when I'd been too young to understand sexual desire, I'd always wanted to be near Ethan. *My* Ethan. And I wasn't going to let a single second longer pass without him knowing that.

"I'm staying with you." Where I belonged.

He stared at me, and for one horrible moment, I thought he was going to turn me down.

"I'm not going anywhere without you, Ethan. You hear me?"

His nod calmed me down. It was a gesture I was familiar with: a slow, solemn gesture that told me he was absorbing and processing. Taking everything in.

"Okay," he finally said.

"Can Alena come with us too? The kidnappers were the worst to her. You saw. I'm worried about her. She might need to be around someone she can trust."

"We're going to have to walk about five miles. Can she make it?"

I nodded. "Yes. I know she can."

"Okay then. Let me tell Isaac and Landon."

He ducked away from me to talk to them, so I was the one who shook Alena gently awake beside me. "Hey girl. You okay? It's time to go."

She winced. "Yeah, I think so."

"Are you okay to walk? We have about five miles to go."

"Yeah. My leg is feeling better. But I—" she faded off.

I pulled her in for a gentle hug. "Don't think about anything now. Let's just get out of here."

At the barn door, the three others on Ethan's team and Russell and Susan were gathered together. They slipped out one by one, and Russell was last, turning to give me a wave before he disappeared into the darkness.

"What's going on?" Alena asked.

"The car they found won't fit everyone. You, Ethan, and I are going to the next town to steal another one. I want us to stay together."

Alena leaned in closer. "Me too."

Ethan came over. "Ready, ladies?"

We both nodded.

He was in mission mode again, that same badass posture that I'd seen when he'd broken into my cell. "Follow my lead and be as quiet as possible. Let me know if we need to stop."

Ethan helped us to our feet, and we followed him to the door. There was nothing we had to take with us. Ethan had a small pack with what was left of the food and water. Other than the locket, nothing else was important.

Ethan rushed us across the open space between the barn and the tree line without letting us slow down. It was colder now, though it was in the middle of summer. The buildings where they'd kept us had been cool but not cold. Possibly there was heating, or maybe the thickness of the old stone had acted as a natural insulator against the cold.

The temperature was far lower than what I would expect for summer. So that meant we were at a higher altitude. They had taken us into the mountains. That might cause some problems for getting out. The mountains were more isolated and sparsely populated.

We kept to the shadows of the trees whenever the moon came out from behind the dense clouds. Ethan took the lead. I hung back with Alena, helping her stay as silent as possible in case anyone was around in the woods.

It wasn't easy. I'd had training in stealth and how to hide—a byproduct of growing up in the Wyoming wilderness and it having nearly killed me more than once—but she'd lived in cities all her life, plus she was still injured. We followed Ethan's steps as carefully as possible. He was definitely moving much slower because of us.

All things considered, it went smoothly. I was entirely focused on the movement and had no concept of how far we had gone. All I knew was that the temperature continued to drop, and if there'd been more than a scrap of light, I would have been able to see my breath.

Ethan kept moving ahead, then circling back to us. I knew he was looking out for any danger on all sides. I kept pace with Alena. It was clear that she wasn't moving as quickly as Ethan wanted her to, but he was always quick to help and encourage her when she stumbled.

Of course he would encourage her. That was who Ethan was. He was kind and gentle and always had been. Quiet, strong, and steady. My Ethan.

A few minutes later, he stopped short, and I immediately grabbed Alena to a halt also. He backed us up quickly, retreating a few hundred feet to deeper shadows before pulling us closer to one of the large trees.

Ethan yanked me against his body, pinning me between him and the tree. I pulled Alena next to me also. She started to speak, and I slammed a hand over her mouth, shaking my head.

Ethan had heard or seen something we hadn't.

My heart pounded against my chest in the darkness, ears straining for what had made us hide. And then I heard it. Slow, steady, crunching footsteps through the trees. My breath went shallow. We couldn't afford to be taken back. Alena wouldn't survive much more mistreatment.

Ethan's arms tightened around me. It was okay. He was here. He wasn't going to let them take us. I pulled Alena closer too.

Another set of footsteps, and then another. The group slowly passed by us. Too slowly. They were searching, like they'd been tipped off that we were on the run again and in this area.

In the darkness, I could see a shape, but I didn't dare move. Ethan's fingers tightened around me and Alena grabbed my hand in a death grip until they were gone.

We stayed still until the footsteps were long faded. Finally Ethan let me go.

"Let's move," he whispered. "Quickly."

We did. Faster than we had before. Alena didn't complain, and she did her best to not slow us down. None of us spoke or lost focus, just moved through trees until we could see lights on the horizon. There was the town.

But that didn't mean much. We were still exposed, still needed to find a car.

We kept moving until we were on the outskirts, then slowly moved along the perimeter of the town. Alena's limp was growing worse as we moved. The walk had taken its toll, and we needed to stop soon. While it had gotten colder, it had also grown damp, and we were all dragging.

"Ethan," I whispered. He turned back and joined me. "She can't go much farther."

He nodded and turned away and that feeling of distance between us built again. I knew he was focused on getting us out of danger, but I also knew that we were out of sync. On the same side, but not a *team*. And I absolutely hated it. Hated myself because I'd caused it.

"Here," Ethan said softly from a short distance ahead. He led us to a small building that was little more than a shed, but it was dry and clean enough. It would do.

I helped Alena inside, and she stifled a groan as she sat down.

"You all right?"

"I'll live."

Ethan took off the pack. "There's more food in there. We'll rest of a couple of hours and then find a car to get the hell out of here."

"Sounds good to me," Alena said.

"Do you want something to eat?" I asked her as we both took in some water.

She shook her head. "No, just sleep."

I grabbed a granola bar out of the pack before pushing it toward her. "Use that as a pillow. Get some sleep."

"What about you?"

"I'll manage," I smiled.

And I would. But I didn't plan on sleeping, even if I might need it. Because finally, Ethan and I were as alone as we were going to get, and I needed to clear the air.

Alena curled up with the backpack, and it was only minutes before her breathing became soft and even. Ethan sat in the door of the shed, ever watchful. But he was aware of me as I came up beside him.

It was time to do this. It was time for me to tell Ethan the truth and hope it would be enough.

CHAPTER THIRTEEN

Jess

"She's asleep," I said. "Is this a good time to talk? About everything?"

Ethan and I both leaned against opposite sides of the door-frame, so close and yet so distant it felt like agony.

My fault.

He looked at me, and I felt the full weight of that stare. Ethan had the ability to look at you in a way no one else could. He could pin you to the spot or make you feel completely full of life, and all it took was one glance.

Right now, I was pinned. Not what I wanted.

"Does *everything* include the research that's missing from the Vandercroft biotech lab?" he asked. "Because I definitely have some questions about that."

My heart threw itself against my ribs. "How do you know about that?"

Ethan smiled a little. "It's how we got a team here so quickly

—there's pressure from pretty high up to make sure that research doesn't fall into the wrong hands."

"Oh."

"Somebody would have come for you anyway, with three of the four of you having high-profile parents. But Vandercroft realized some top secret data had been taken, research co-funded by Uncle Sam, and that it looked like one of the American kids had done it."

Shit. Now telling him what I'd done might look like I was covering my own tracks.

How had I not calculated this? It seemed obvious now that given the nature of the research, the military and government would already be tracking it.

The kinds of things my team had been developing at Vandercroft, the strides we'd made in biotechnology over the past two years . . . they were primed to change the world. Or potentially end it if that information got into the wrong hands. It made sense that the heads of the fellowship program would have taken their knowledge of the theft to someone higher up the chain.

I rubbed the bridge of my nose with my fingers, trying to ease some of the tension there. Sometimes, I got way too far into my own head. I thought I was the only one who could fix something because I had obviously thought of everything, and all I did was end up making things worse.

I opened my mouth to speak, but before I could, he slid closer. He was so close to me now that I could feel his body heat, though he still wasn't touching me. I couldn't breathe with him this close. After months of distance and tension, all I wanted was to sink into his arms and let him hold me. Touch me. Everything.

"I need the answer to one question, Jess," he whispered. "And it has to be the truth."

"Anything," I said. I never lied to Ethan. I left things out on occasion, but I could never stomach lying to him. He'd been able to see through me since we were kids.

"Once we get out of this country, do I need to take you somewhere no one will find us?"

He hadn't asked if I'd done it or why. He'd asked if he had to take me somewhere to keep from getting arrested for treason. Which meant that he wasn't planning to leave me, even if I'd committed the crime.

I closed my eyes as relief flooded through me. Maybe there wasn't quite as much distance as I thought. "You would really do that? Run away with me, even if I'm guilty? Even after . . . what you saw with Russell?"

Ethan's hand came up and wrapped behind my neck. He wove his fingers into my hair. His forehead rested against mine.

"Yes," he breathed. "I would do that for you. I would do anything for you, Jess. Anything to keep you safe. Even if that means protecting you from yourself."

I knew what going on the run would mean. It would mean giving up his entire life for me. His career in the Navy. And the fact that he was willing to do that without question . . . it took my breath away.

"Uncle Ian has already made a plan," he said. "It's all ready to go if that's what needs to happen. So you need to tell me Jess, do we need to run? Did you take the research?"

I bit my lip. "Yes."

He sighed, eyes closing. His shoulders tightened, but he didn't pull away from me. "Okay, then we—"

"But I didn't take it to steal it. I took it to keep it from being stolen. Someone was—*is*—planning on selling it, and I didn't want to take the chance that they would move before I had a plan. So I left a dummy copy to be stolen, and I have the real research."

He yanked me against his chest, wrapping his arms around

me. "You're going to be the death of me, woman. When Ian told me you were on the list of suspects, I told him that it couldn't be you, or if it was, it was because of something we didn't know. Something like this."

I breathed in his scent, happy to finally be in his arms where I belonged.

Ethan hadn't doubted me. That made everything okay.

"I've been working on this for months. I've narrowed down the list of suspects to Russell or Susan. I've been trying to get closer to them in order to find out more."

"Why?" He stepped back so we could see each other. "Why not go directly to the research heads at Vandercroft? Or the authorities?"

"I should have," I said quietly. "But I knew all our research would get shut down for months if there was a full investigation. The stuff we're working on, Ethan, it's just . . . amazing. And we needed all our time to keep it moving forward. I thought I could handle it. Narrow it down, catch the thief, and turn them in, and then the rest of the team would never have a hiccup in their work."

"Jess." He sounded both exasperated and amused. It wasn't the first time I'd heard that particular tone as he said my name.

"I know. I'm sorry. I should have told someone. At least Alena." Looking over, I could tell that she was still completely asleep. "She probably could have helped me watch Susan and Russell. Helped me figure it out faster without halting the program at all."

He shook his head. "That big brain of yours gets you in trouble sometimes. You try to handle too much yourself."

I grimaced. "This whole trip was to draw them out. I was hoping they'd do something to give me a clue which one was the culprit. I don't know, maybe make up a bullshit reason to get back to London early or something. Anything. Obviously, it didn't end up that way."

Ethan stepped back a little, and I wanted to grab him and pull him back to me. "Is that what your birthday was about? You were trying to charm Russell to get information?"

I shook my head. "I can't believe you were there and didn't tell me. I would've much rather have been with you than scoping out Russell. I thought you were in Africa."

"No, Germany. They approved my request for leave at the last minute, and I wanted to surprise you." He glanced outside as a lookout for a moment before turning back to me. "Ends up I was the one who got surprised."

"It wasn't real, I promise. I was trying to get Russell to trust me, maybe confide in me." I stepped forward into his space. "I swear to you, Ethan, there is no part of me that wants Russell Kramer. I only want you."

He was silent for so long, studying the landscape out the doorway, I thought he might not say anything at all. I finally reached out and touched his forearm.

"Are you sure?" he finally asked.

"What?" I gasped. "Why would you ask that?"

He shrugged. "Seeing you with him that way made me think maybe you wanted to branch out and . . ." He scrubbed his hand over his face. "Jesus, I don't know. Try other people? We've been together since you were in preschool, Jess. How can you be sure that I'm the one that you want?"

In all the time that I'd known Ethan, I'd never heard him sound like this. The resignation in his voice had panic bubbling up inside me.

I didn't want to *try* anyone else. I wanted Ethan. Only him. There'd never been a doubt in my mind.

But he was right. We'd been together forever. Maybe I wasn't the one having second thoughts.

"Is that what you want? To—" I choked on the words. "To try other women?"

The very idea of that made me want to scream. Made me

sick. Imagining him with anyone else was devastating in a way that I was not prepared for. And the reaction that I was having, and barely in control of, only solidified my knowledge that I didn't want anyone other than him.

But if that was what he needed . . . I could survive it. Because even if it was what he decided to do, Ethan would find his way back to me. He always did.

He'd found his way to me in the middle of this hellish nightmare, and I knew that he would do it again. We were meant to be together. Forever. No matter what happened along the way.

Ethan grabbed my hand. "No, that's not what I want. But . . . now might not be the best time to be talking about our future. Neither of us is in the right frame of mind."

It wasn't exactly a comforting statement, but I saw the logic in it. In order for us to have a future together, we had to survive the present. And that meant getting past armed bad guys and making sure that I didn't go to jail for treason and espionage.

But I still wanted to talk about it. To clear the air. To tell him I wanted *only* him and pray he'd say the same.

Ethan and I had always been in sync. Like a heartbeat. He was the first beat and I was the second. Being out of rhythm with him was like having sandpaper under my skin. Constant friction and anxiety.

"Let's focus on now," he said again. "Getting out of this. Isaac and Landon work for Ian. And they know about the research. They're going to be looking for anything out of the ordinary or suspicious with Russell and Susan."

"Okay," I whispered. It was at least good to have someone I could talk to about this.

"Russell in particular because his father sent MacQueen. Guy feels a little sketchy."

"That was why Isaac and Landon both had to go with MacQueen instead of splitting us in half?" I asked.

Ethan nodded.

"What's the concern?"

His mouth set in a firm line, and I knew the expression. He was either deciding what was okay to tell me or finding a way to make something awful sound better. "Nigel Kramer, Russell's dad, forced MacQueen onto the team at the last minute. And because of how determined he was to have his man with us, we think it might be because he's not only concerned about his son's safety."

"So maybe I was right about him."

Ethan nodded. "There's every chance Nigel could be in on stealing the research with Russell. Or the one pressuring his son to do it. Until we're sure that's not the case, we'll be watching MacQueen."

I reached up and tapped my locket. "Don't worry. The real research is safe. No chance it falls into the wrong hands while I have it."

His eyes narrowed as he made the connection. He nodded. "Good."

"Why are you here with Uncle Ian's men rather than your SEAL team?"

He glanced away. "As of a few days ago, I'm not active duty anymore. I'm reserves."

My eyes bugged wide. "What? Why?"

He shrugged. "A couple of months ago, it was time to decide whether to re-up, and I decided I didn't want to stay active duty. I always knew I wasn't a lifer."

Given everything, I had no right to be hurt that he hadn't discussed this with me, but I still was. "Wow. I can't believe you didn't mention it to me. I mean, you don't have to ask my permission, but I feel like this was something we should've talked through together."

Unless . . . his future plans no longer included me. I had to swallow my panic at the thought. No. Things could not have gotten that bad so quickly.

He stiffened. "I'd planned to talk to you, but . . ."

He'd made this decision a couple of months ago, so that meant . . . "When you came to London for my birthday?"

"Yes. I'd planned to talk to you then, but we didn't get a chance."

"Ethan." I reached out to touch his arm again. He didn't pull away, that was good. "I'm so sorry. I hope you didn't make any choices because of what you saw that night."

He shrugged one shoulder. "I did, but it was a choice I needed to make anyway."

I wanted to ask him more about it but he stopped me before I could.

"Look, we should get some rest," he said softly. "We've got to get going again soon."

I nodded, and he closed the door to the shed, locking us in deeper darkness. We walked closer to where Alena was sleeping and lay down on the ground.

Despair threatened to swallow me. The situation was so much worse than I'd thought. I'd thought we were in danger, that we might die at the hands of Radu and his men. That should've been bad enough.

But finding out that I might have created some emotional chasm between Ethan and me? That was worse than facing kidnappers with giant guns.

Tears leaked out of my eyes as I lay there in the darkness, trying not to sob. I couldn't do this, not without Ethan. So he cared enough about me to get me somewhere safe if I were guilty. But it wasn't enough. I needed his *love*.

I started to hyperventilate. I was going to have to sit up to get myself under control, beg Ethan to give me another chance.

Then, as if he could feel my panic, feel my need for him, his hand reached over and linked with mine.

It was enough. I wanted so much more, but having his fingers clutched in my own was enough to ground me. Center me.

I knew one thing for certain: I wasn't letting go.

CHAPTER FOURTEEN

SIXTEEN YEARS AGO
Ethan - 8
Jess - 5

ETHAN WAS in so much trouble.

He was supposed be home with Skywalker before the rain came. But he and Jess had been having so much fun playing with the dog that he couldn't do it. And then Skywalker had seen a rabbit or something and run away. Ethan and Jess had run after him.

Ethan had spent enough time in the woods to know where they were, but he didn't know where Skywalker was. They'd been looking for him for more than thirty minutes now. The rain was starting to come harder.

He looked over at Jess. "Maybe we should just go home."

Jess grabbed his hand. "Not without Skywalker. We'll find him. Don't worry."

They kept walking and calling for the dog. Ethan should

have never let him off the leash. After a few more minutes, he knew they were getting too far away from everything. It was time to turn around and go back home.

Ethan couldn't stand the thought of his dog out in a storm like this, but he had to think of Jess. It was more important to keep her safe. She trusted him. And they were almost to the part of the woods that led up from the river embankment. Dad said they weren't allowed to go there without adults. It was too dangerous.

He reached out a hand for Jess to stop. "It's time to go home. We can't go any farther. We'll have to look for Skywalker later."

Her eyes were wide. "But—"

"Hey, are you kids looking for a dog?" Ethan spun around at the sound of a man's voice behind them.

He immediately took Jess and pulled her so he was between her and the man. Ethan wasn't scared of strangers, but if this person was bad, he wanted to be able to protect Jess.

But the guy didn't look bad. He had on hiking gear and had some hunter's weapons. They got a lot of hikers and hunters around here.

"Yes, sir," Ethan told him. "Our dog, Skywalker, ran away, and we're trying to find him."

The man pointed farther up the hill. "I saw a dog up there a few minutes ago. You can probably catch him if you hurry."

"Okay. Thank you."

The man turned the other way and began walking. That made Ethan feel better. He was just trying to help them. There was no need to be afraid.

They weren't supposed to go up that hill, but if they were this close, he had to try to bring Skywalker home.

"You stay here, and I'll climb up the hill and see if I can find him," he told Jess.

She shook her head rapidly. "No, I want to go with you. Don't leave me here, please, E. I'll be scared."

Ethan studied her with narrowed eyes. Jess did not tend to get scared even in situations where someone should be scared. But he didn't want to leave her behind either. "Okay, but let's hurry. This rain is getting worse."

They scurried up the embankment the best they could. The soil was much looser here, and there were pebbles sliding from farther above them, slippery from mud. This was part of the reason Dad had always said this place was off-limits. The ground could get too loose and cause landslides.

But what would a landslide do to Skywalker? He wouldn't know to get out of the way.

"Skywalker!" Ethan yelled. Jess joined him, also calling for the dog.

Another fifteen minutes passed and still there was no sign of him. Ethan glanced around and realized they were in trouble. They'd come up too far, and the rain was too hard now. Going back down the way they'd come wasn't an option. He reached over and grabbed Jess's hand.

"We're going to have to go up a little farther. There's a cut-through on the side of the hill where we can take shelter. We've got to get out of this rain, Jess."

"Okay," she said. "I'm cold."

They both had on jackets, but they've been out in the rain so long they were soaked through. They hadn't expected to be out this long.

"Come on, we'll get to the cut-through. It'll be warmer, and there won't be so much wind. Okay?"

Jess nodded her little head. "Okay."

Ethan tried to hurry, but at the same time he was very careful. More and more of the rocks and dirt were sliding as they stepped. He kept hold of Jess's hand. He didn't want to fall.

They almost made it. He could almost see the cut-through when Jess let out a little scream.

"Rocks, Ethan. Rocks!"

He spun and saw the rocks farther up the hill, not rolling, but sliding down in mud that had loosened. There was no way that they were going to be able to get out of their path. Ethan put his arms around Jess and pulled her up against him as the mud began to slide under their feet.

They fell. He protected her with his body as much as he could, trying not to cry out as the rocks hit him in his back. But he couldn't stop the scream that fell from his lips as a large rock rolled onto his ankle and stopped there.

"Ethan, Ethan, are you okay?" Jess scrambled away from him when the mudslide stopped.

Ethan was trying just to breathe. There were a bunch of rocks on his legs now. None as big as the one on his ankle. The pain rolled over him in waves, and he was afraid he was going to throw up. He couldn't move his leg at all.

Now what was he going to do? What was Jess going to do? She didn't know how to get home. How were they going to get home?

He started to cry.

Jess threw her arms around his neck. "No, Ethan. Don't cry. I'll help get the rocks off your leg. I'll help you."

She moved all the little rocks she could manage, and he forced himself to be quiet, even though it hurt really bad. But when it came to the big rock, there was no way she was going to be able to pick that up. Ethan couldn't do it either. And even if he could, he didn't think he was going to be able to walk. He was breathing hard just sitting there. He lay back down.

"Jess, I need you to keep going up the hill a little bit to the cut-through. It will be dry in there, and you can get warm."

Her big bottom lip started to quiver. "But I don't want to go by myself."

"You have to. I don't think that I can get up."

"Then I'm staying here with you," she whispered.

He couldn't let Jess stay out in the cold. He sat back up and using every bit of strength he had, he tried to move his leg from under the rock. He couldn't do it. He couldn't move it.

And a second later, he couldn't keep everything around him from turning black.

JESS TRIED NOT TO CRY. She tried not to cry most of the time, even though her mom had told her it was okay to cry sometimes.

Crying was for babies. Jess may only be five years old, but she wasn't a baby. It was better to think of a way out of a problem than to sit and cry about it.

But Ethan was taking a nap. Ethan never took a nap, and the big rock was on his leg, and he was hurt bad. And she was so cold, she wanted to cry. She didn't, but she wanted to.

"Ethan, please wake up." She knelt by his head and touched his cheek. "Please wake up."

She needed to find some sort of branch that she could use as a lever for moving the rock. Mrs. Pearl had made her study and build one in school when she'd gotten bored.

But there weren't branches around, and she didn't want to leave Ethan. What if a rock fell on his head like it had his leg?

So she stayed. She yelled for help as loud as she could, hoping the man who'd seen Skywalker might hear her and come back. She wasn't supposed to talk to strangers, but she would if that man could get Ethan out. But he didn't come back.

She covered Ethan when small rocks slid their way and tried to keep his face dry in the rain.

"Jess, you have to go." He said the same thing every time he woke up.

She said the same thing too. "I'm not going to leave you. I'll never leave you."

Eventually, Jess did cry. She was cold and hungry and tired and Ethan wouldn't stay awake very long. She knew that wasn't good.

And she cried because she didn't know what to do. She was smarter than almost everyone—Mama said being smarter didn't make her better, and that being smart was a responsibility—but she couldn't figure out what to do.

But mostly she cried because what if Ethan died here? She couldn't live without her Ethan.

She was lying next to him when she heard someone calling their names. At first she thought she was dreaming since it was a woman.

"Mama?" It didn't sound like her. She couldn't see anybody in the rain.

"Jess! Keep yelling, sweetie. I'm going to help you. Can you sing the alphabet really loud?"

Uh, yeah, she could do it backward just as easily. She started singing.

"You're doing great, kiddo. Keep going."

Jess saw the woman a few minutes later. Short with blond hair. "You're not my mommy."

"Yeah, sweetie, I'm sorry. I'm Ray."

"Uncle Dorian's girlfriend." She didn't talk much. But Uncle Dorian didn't talk much either.

"Yeah. I'm his girlfriend. I'm here to get you back to your mom."

Good. "Ethan's hurt bad."

"He's going to be okay."

She almost started crying again. "I've been trying to keep the rain off of him as much as I could while he was sleeping. I wasn't strong enough to move the rocks. And I didn't know my way home to go get help. And I'm afraid Skywalker is hurt."

"No, Skywalker made it back to Ethan's house. That's how we knew you guys were in trouble. And you did the right thing staying here with him. He might've been scared without you."

Skywalker was safe, and she'd done the right thing. And Uncle Dorian's girlfriend with the boy's name was going to help. That was all that mattered.

Jess was tired and cold and wanted to go home. "This cave has a cut-through to the other side. Ethan was trying to get us there when the rocks fell."

"How long has Ethan been sleeping?"

"He wakes up and talks to me but then goes back to sleep." She wanted her Ethan to wake up and talk to her.

"I'm going to move some of these rocks you couldn't lift, and we're going to take Ethan out through the other side of the cavern, okay?"

Jess nodded. "But you're hurt too." She pointed at Ray's face where her nose was bleeding. Maybe rocks had fallen on her too.

Ray winked at her. "Just a nosebleed, nothing to worry about. Let's focus on Ethan."

Ray started moving rocks, and Jess tried to help but her hands were so cold she couldn't even hold the rocks.

"You know what?" Ray winked at her. "Let's get you inside the cavern, and I'll get Ethan. I think that will be the easiest way."

She didn't want to leave Ethan, but she was smart enough to know she was slowing Ray down, so she nodded, and they went inside the cavern. Being out of the wind and rain felt *so good*.

"Be careful of the rocks," Jess said as Ray turned to go back out. "I knew I had to protect Ethan from the rocks."

"I'm not going to let any rocks get your boy."

Jess nodded. Uncle Dorian was amazing, and he would have a girlfriend who was amazing too. She would help Ethan.

And Jess would never let anything happen to him ever again.

CHAPTER FIFTEEN

ETHAN

TIME PASSED SLOWLY. I held myself still next to Jess for what must have been more than an hour. She was sleeping, but I had no plans to. I needed to keep watch, be ready to make a move if we were discovered.

But even if that weren't the case, the chance to lie next to her and hold her hand wasn't something I was going to miss for something as mundane as sleeping.

She'd been about to lose it earlier. I had felt it on a level that was attuned to only her. All I could offer her was my hand, but I'd been glad when she'd taken it. Glad that the connection between us had been reestablished.

Jess's hand curled tighter into mine in sleep, and I held on. One hand on her, the other on my weapon. I was listening for any kind of movement outside the shed that would tell me that we'd been found, but there was nothing. It was strangely peaceful here.

Until there was movement, but not outside.

Alena rose from where she had been sleeping and crept toward the door. I didn't move. Not until she had slipped out the door behind me, and then I gently eased myself away from Jess.

Odds were that Alena was going to the bathroom, but I was still going to watch her back. She shouldn't have gone out alone, but maybe she was embarrassed to ask one of us to come with her. But with Radu and his men combing the woods, we couldn't be too careful.

Alena was standing outside the door, and I was about to let her know I was there, when she started to run. My instincts screamed. This wasn't the kind of run that spoke of embarrassment or needing to relieve yourself. This was the kind of run you used to get distance.

She was running away from us.

I didn't want to leave Jess alone, but I couldn't let Alena leave like this. Something was very wrong. I'd seen the girl limping with every step we'd traveled. She'd been clumsy and loud, clearly injured. And now she was sprinting at full speed? That didn't add up. And given what was at stake, we couldn't take any chances.

Shutting the door behind me, I followed Alena in the direction that she'd gone, cutting wide so there was less chance she would detect me. I moved silently through the trees until I spotted her. She hadn't gone far. Far enough that neither Jess nor I would be able to see or hear her, but no farther.

A light appeared, illuminating her face. She had a working cell phone. Not only that, but one that worked in Moldova—not something a broke Vandercroft student would have. I crept closer as she lifted the phone to her ear. Whoever she was calling, I needed to know what she telling them.

"Yeah, I'm sorry," she said in English. "There hasn't been any time for me to get away before now. We've split into two groups, five and three. The group of five already has a vehicle and is heading to their backup rendezvous. Should be about twenty miles northwest of the farm. Don't know the exact location, but should get you close enough. They're going to wait for us."

She listened for a minute. "You should have some time. We don't have a vehicle yet, and I'm faking an injury. I can slow them down to buy you more."

A brief silence, and then a laugh. "Neither Russell nor Susan had it. You're not going to believe this. Jess had it the entire time. I never suspected the sneaky bitch. She's honestly better than I gave her credit for."

Anger burned in my chest, but I held myself still. Jess considered Alena one of her closest friends. Hadn't suspected her at all. This would hurt Jess.

What was Alena's motivation here? She was a part of one of the most prestigious biotech research teams in the world. Everyone who was a part of it, including Alena, was a certified genius. I didn't pretend to understand why she would give up a bright future like that.

"I don't know where it is," Alena said. "But I'll find out. Then you'll have to get to it immediately."

Whatever instinct had made Jess not say where she was hiding the research out loud, I thanked the universe for it. It might have saved both of our lives. If Alena was hiding a phone, was she also hiding a weapon? If she was willing to betray her best friend, was she willing to kill?

I wasn't going to wait to find definitive answers.

"We're just outside the town, five miles from the farm," she said. "Oh, you're that close? Damn, yeah. We're in a little shed on the south side, shouldn't be too hard to find." Alena laughed. "All right, see you in ten minutes."

Ten minutes? Fuck. We had to move. Ten minutes was far too close if Jess and I had any chance of getting away from whoever was on the other end of the phone.

I didn't hesitate. In one smooth movement, I pulled my tranquilizer gun and fired. Alena never saw the dart coming as it buried itself in her neck. I only stayed long enough to see that she hit the ground and was fully unconscious, and then I ran.

My only goal now was to get Jess out of here. When I'd told her that I would do anything to keep her safe, I'd been telling the truth.

But ten minutes wasn't much time, and the enemy knew our exact location. I tried to keep myself quiet so I didn't draw any extra attention and scare Jess, but that was weighed against my need for speed at all costs.

I pushed into the shed and dropped to my knees beside Jess. The movement had her opening her eyes, like always. Our entire lives Jess had been the kind of person to wake up quickly, fully awake. I'd always been jealous of that ability, but I was desperately grateful for it now.

"What's going on?"

"We have to go," I said, pulling her to her feet and grabbing the backpack from where Alena had left it. "Now. They know where we are, and they'll be here in minutes."

I took her hand and pulled her out the door. "Wait," she yanked me back, "Where's Alena?"

"Jess, I'm sorry. She's the traitor."

The pain that flooded her features gutted me. "What?"

"I know," I said, taking her face in my hands. "I know, and I'm sorry. I'll tell you everything. But right now, we have to move because she called her bad guy friends, and they're incoming."

She nodded, and I pulled her forward again, running toward the town. We needed cover, and right now, buildings were a good bet. Plus, the two of us together were far less conspicuous. We could maybe blend in, or pretend to be two lovers out late.

Jess had no problem keeping up, following my lead and obeying the signals that I gave her. The town was quiet, most everyone sleeping but us. It was a relief, but it was also nerve-wracking because any sound could give us away.

We needed to get enough distance to hide and call Isaac and Landon. They needed to know about Alena, if only because they could stop keeping as close an eye on MacQueen and the others.

My mind traced the thought, and I had to admit that it was still possible that Nigel Kramer was behind all of it. Maybe he'd thought it would be easier to use someone in the fellowship program who couldn't be connected to him. It would be smart, since everyone would assume that if he was involved, Russell would be as well. If Russell was proven innocent, Nigel would look innocent by association.

Jess and I didn't stop moving until we were on the far side of the town and once again in the trees. We stopped in a small clearing and listened. The night was entirely silent. We were far enough to risk it, and we didn't have much of a choice.

I pulled out the phone I had on me. It was for emergencies only, and this qualified. We weren't authorized to be in the country, and the first thing we'd learned on missions was never to assume people wouldn't be listening.

Given the research and the kind of people who would be after it, we would be foolish to assume that whoever wanted it didn't have resources.

The phone signal was weak, but I got enough to make the call. Isaac answered on the third ring. "Bollinger. Everything all right?"

"No. If you're at the rendezvous point, leave. Alena is the traitor. She was faking her injuries."

"Fuck," Isaac said. "Does she have the research?"

"No. It's safe for now. But Alena called people in on both of

123

our locations. Jess and I made it away, but they will be coming for you."

A violent curse came from the other end of the line. "We never made it. Radu has the local police in his pocket. There are roadblocks everywhere. We've already had to switch cars. But we were still trying to make it to the point."

"Yeah," I said. "It's burned. What's the plan?"

He sighed, and I waited as he relayed the information to Landon. They discussed for a moment, and I took a breath. My instincts were telling me to move. But we needed a plan first.

"He expects us to be heading north," Isaac said. "So we'll double back and head south to Romania. We can meet you on the way."

My mind went into overdrive, rifling through maps in my head and judging distances. There was more at play here now, knowing that Radu had contacts with law enforcement and that Jess had the research on her person—something that I wasn't going to tell them over a phone in hostile territory.

"We'll still have trouble getting a vehicle for seven," I said, "and we're still conspicuous. Jess and I can travel faster together. It's better to stay split." Yes. This was the right call. I would keep Jess safe.

"Are you sure?"

"I am. We'll get to Kishinev, and I'll have Ian arrange an extraction there." The capital city would provide a lot more options.

Isaac made a sound of hesitation. "That's a long way to go, Ethan. Can Jess handle that kind of trip?"

"Absolutely." I wasn't going to elaborate, but my Jess could handle anything thrown at her. They hadn't seen her ready to take down the kidnapper who was entering her room in order to save her friend. Her friend who had betrayed her.

"Okay," Isaac said. "Get moving. Check in if you need to."

"Will do."

I hung up and looked at Jess.

"Kishinev?" she asked.

"Yeah. The others will head to the Romanian border."

Now that I had a goal, I could think my way through. I didn't want to go back toward the town and the danger, but we needed clothes that would help us blend in better. I'd seen some hanging behind one of the houses we'd passed, and in several other yards. Maybe something there would fit us.

"Clothes," I whispered before leading her back the way we came.

It didn't take long to find things. Luck was on our side for once. Plain jeans and a T-shirt for me, and the same for Jess, along with a sweater.

But her hair would be a dead giveaway for the people looking for us. That white blonde could be seen a long way off. As we were moving away from the town again, I grabbed a scarf for her to cover it. It was way too cold out here, but we had no choice but to change as quickly as possible in the darkness.

I grabbed the map I'd stuffed into the pack earlier. My memory was good, but I wasn't taking chances. I needed to get Jess as far away from here as possible as fast as possible.

And it was a distraction from the fact that Jess was changing just feet from me. Now wasn't the time to think about how badly I wanted her, but it was Jess. And I was aching to touch her.

I was focused on the map, looking for the fastest path to Kishinev, when Jess and I both froze. The low sound of a train horn echoed through the air. It was a mournful sound, and the best damn thing that I'd ever heard in my life. The horn sounded again, and a third time. All in the same general direction.

That meant it wasn't moving quickly. Could be a freight train, which would be perfect, if it was going our way.

Using the light from my phone screen at its lowest brightness, I found the tracks on the map. Jess pointed to the paper. "There."

She'd found where the tracks bent closest to us. Not far. Maybe a mile. "We'll have to run."

"I'm ready."

I shoved the map back into the backpack and lifted it onto my shoulders. "Let's go."

We didn't bother with silence, running through the trees as fast as we could go. Adrenaline pumped in my veins, and it drove me faster. I knew it drove Jess too. We had to catch that train.

We came to the edge of the tree line as the train passed us slowly on the tracks. We hadn't missed it, but the end was coming.

Together, we ran for the nearest car. I pushed for one more burst of speed, leaping onto the car so that I could turn and reach for Jess. She jumped for my hand, and I caught her, lifting her into my arms and to safety.

We pulled open the door on the train car and tumbled inside together before closing it behind us. And somehow, Jess was in my arms again, just like I wanted her to be. We were safe.

For now.

CHAPTER SIXTEEN

ETHAN

THE FIRST THING I did was check out the car to make sure we were alone. It was a freight car, and I wasn't expecting any company, but we may not be the only people who saw the train as a free means of travel.

But we were alone.

I sat back down next to Jess near the rear of the car next to some crates. For a long time, we didn't move. We were both breathing heavily after our frantic run, but we had made it.

It didn't take long to get damned cold once we weren't moving anymore. We sat together, leaning against the wall of the car as far from the door as we could so less freezing air would leak in. Jess rested her head on my shoulder, and I held her close.

I wished that we were anywhere else—that this was something we were doing when we were calmly on vacation and not running for our lives. But given the circumstances, I would take what I could get.

We were alive, we were relatively safe, and Jess wasn't a traitor.

I'd never believed she was, but hearing her tell me what had happened—including why she'd been flirting with Russell—finally eased the weight that had been sitting on my chest.

Yes, she'd gotten herself in trouble, but not because she'd done something bad, but because she'd been trying to do something good. That was just who she was.

I dozed with her next to me. This was the first time I'd felt safe enough to truly relax. No one was going to come into the car unnoticed—not if they had to pull the car door open. And with Jess's warmth . . .

It must have been a couple hours when her voice had me on high alert. I startled awake, ready to jump, but Jess held me back.

"It's fine," she said. "Nothing's wrong."

I rubbed the sleep from my eyes. "Sorry."

She shook her head. "Don't apologize. I'm glad you're ready."

Relaxing against the wall again, I slipped my arm back around her. Jess's voice was soft against the noise of the train car, but this close, I could still hear her.

"When I was alone in that room, hurt and chained . . . all I could think about was how I wanted you there. I wanted you to come and rescue me." She paused. "And then you showed up."

"I will always show up. Every single time." And I meant it. Whether she wanted me to or not.

Suddenly, she seemed too far away despite being next to each other. I slipped both arms around her and lifted her so she was sitting on my lap. She cuddled against me, her hand resting on my chest, over my heart.

We both relaxed as if we were finally where we belonged.

"I don't understand how she could do this," Jess whispered.

"Alena?"

"Yeah." Her voice was full of sadness. "And I don't know how I didn't see it."

"She's a good actress. Clearly."

"But why? Money? She betrayed everything we've worked so hard for. Betrayed our country." The next words were even quieter. "Betrayed me. Why?"

I tightened my arms around her. "I don't know."

"Months. I've spent months trying to track who wanted to steal the research. I looked at Alena peripherally, but obviously not close enough. How could I have been so stupid?"

I tucked her head under my chin. "You know you're not stupid. You trusted her. You weren't looking for her connection."

"But I still should have seen it."

I stroked my hand down her beautiful blonde hair, loving, as always, the feel of strands on my fingers. "You're one person, Jess. You don't have to carry the weight of this all on your own."

"I just—"

"She was in your blind spot." I slipped my hand behind her neck. "Because she's your friend. There's nothing wrong with that."

"Look where we are, Ethan. If I had paid more attention, none of this would have happened."

I reached my arm under her knees and lifted, so she was forced to put the weight of her torso completely on my other arm. I had her semi-helpless and could see her face. "You're a beautiful, trusting soul, and you were betrayed."

In the dim light, her eyes teared. "I should have known something was wrong. I should have—I don't know, been more careful when choosing friends. It was a stupid mistake, one that could have gotten people killed."

"You didn't. What Alena did is not your responsibility. You're not the one who sold her friends out. You're not the one who told them where we could be captured a second time." I pulled her forehead against mine. "It's never a mistake to love someone. And the way you love, Jess—"

I hadn't wanted to get into all of our emotional entanglements until we were safe, but I couldn't stop myself. Didn't want to stop myself.

Having her in my arms, those lips just inches from mine, that silky hair covering my hand . . . I fisted it and was instantly hard, thinking of times I'd fisted it before.

No more distance.

"Your love is like a damn solar flare. When you love, it's bright and warm and complete. And I don't ever want you to lose that. *I* don't want to lose it. Tell me I still have your love."

"You do. Always. Forever. You—"

I couldn't hold myself back anymore. Pulling her lips to mine, I kissed her. It was everything I had missed. Glorious and warm and exactly like stepping into the sunlight.

She gasped against my lips, and I pulled her closer, my tongue invading her mouth. There couldn't be any space between us. Not now. I wasn't going to wait longer when I could finally feel her like this.

I kissed her until we were both breathless and she squirmed against me. But it wasn't enough.

I laid her out on the floor of the train car, holding us together so I could feel all of her pressed against me. My hands explored with a mind of their own, relearning curves that I'd known for years but had been starved of. Jess kissed me back and did her own exploring. I would let her do that as much as she pleased.

This was us. This was where we belonged—as close as possible to each other. All the discord between us evaporated. Our bodies remembered what Ethan and Jess were supposed to be and weren't going to let us hold ourselves apart.

I could admit to myself the relief I felt that Jess had never been with Russell. Not because it would have changed the way I felt—that would never happen. Nor would I have thought less of her for choosing to exercise her choices.

No. I was relieved because the thought of anyone else touching her—anyone else kissing her—drove me mad. It made me feral and possessive. Things I wasn't used to feeling. But imagining anyone else with their hands on her like this? It broke me open.

Jess was mine.

And I was hers.

"Ethan," she whispered. "I need you."

"I'm here."

She groaned. "You know that's not what I meant."

"I—" I hesitated.

"I know that things have been weird, and I know that's my fault. There's a lot we need to talk about. That's fine. I'll talk about whatever you want. But I need you right now. Please."

I paused. My hesitation wasn't because I didn't want her. I wanted her like I wanted oxygen: always. She was just as necessary to me. I'd hesitated because this wasn't the way I wanted our reconciliation to be. I wanted us to be in a bed. Somewhere I could lay her out and worship her body the way it was meant to be worshipped.

But I'd never been able to say no to Jess. Not when it was something that was good for her. Good for us. Not in the seventeen years we'd been together. And never when it was something I wanted just as badly as she did. Maybe more.

I pulled her back up off the floor and into my lap, settling her so she was straddled over my hips. "Yes. But I need you to know this isn't the way I would choose to make love to you. I want to take you slowly. I want to get lost in you and give you so much pleasure you forget your own fucking name. And then I want to do it again. Until neither of us can breathe."

Jess's breath was shallow, and her fingers curled into the fabric of my shirt, clinging to me.

"But that's going to have to wait. Because I need to be inside you right now."

She moaned, leaning in to kiss me again. I took my time. Using my tongue, I teased her lips open, sliding my hands down her back until I could cup her ass and pull her against me. I'd show her exactly how hard she made me—how much I wanted her. If there was nothing else, I wanted her to know that.

CHAPTER SEVENTEEN

Jess

BEING this close to Ethan after so long made me lose my breath. Compared to other couples who'd been together for seventeen years, we didn't have a huge amount of experience together, but that didn't matter. He'd always managed to drive me crazy when we were.

Ethan was a quiet man, but that didn't translate to being quiet in bed. He was devious and inventive and clever. God, I loved him.

The entirety of our long relationship, I had been the loud one. I did most of the talking while he listened and processed. Every word he said was valuable and thought out. But more than that, he let me take the lead. He was happy to be my support in whatever way he could. That was simply who he was. Quiet, steady, and unassuming.

That all changed in the bedroom.

Ethan was the boss there, taking the lead naturally, and I was happy to let him have it. Maybe it was his SEAL training.

Maybe it came from being raised around a dozen alpha hero soldiers.

Maybe it was just who Ethan was on the DNA level.

When we were in bed together, he was determined, focused, and utterly in control. He demanded things of my body that I hadn't known I could give him, and I loved every damned second of it.

Here and now, in the cold on this train, I needed him. More than anything in this world.

Ethan's mouth was on mine, hard and demanding. The way I was sprawled across his lap I could feel how hard he was—that he wanted me too. After everything, just kissing him and knowing that he still wanted me when I could have broken everything . . . it healed something deep down.

"As much as I want you naked," he said, lips moving along my jaw, "we can't risk that."

"I don't care. That's fine. I just need you. Inside me. Right now."

"Are you still on the pill?"

"Yes." And even if I weren't, I didn't care.

Someday I wanted a family with him. And in my mind someday had always been something in the future. What being in this situation had shown me was that I didn't want to wait for anything. I didn't want to hold back or delay on the things that I really cared about, and that was Ethan.

If that meant that we started our family right here in this train car, I didn't give a damn.

He nodded and pushed me back gently, helping me to stand. I didn't realize what he was doing until his hands found my belt and undid it with quick fingers. He didn't need my help, nor did he want it. I was his in this moment, and I would do exactly what he told me to.

I gasped when he stripped my pants and underwear down to my ankles. The air in the car was cold, but Ethan didn't give me a chance to dwell on the temperature. He pulled me to him so I could straddle his lap once more. When I reached between us to find his belt, his hands caught mine. "No. Not yet."

Ethan kissed me hard, tongue darting between my lips to taste me deeper. Every part of me was warm now, falling into the arousal that swam in my veins.

"Put your hands on my shoulders," he whispered. "Don't move them until I tell you to."

"Okay," I breathed, obeying. I savored the feeling of his muscles under my hands and the way they flexed as he moved.

He slipped a hand between us, and suddenly I was gasping for an entirely different reason. I'd grown wet the moment he'd told me he needed to be inside me, but as his fingers brushed across me, I melted.

It had been so long, even the barest touch left me shaking. "Ethan."

"I dreamed about you, you know," he said. "When I was away and we couldn't talk. All I thought about—or dreamed about—was you. Being able to do this." He pushed a finger up inside me, and I moaned. I wasn't a quiet lover. Even with the sound of the moving train I would have to keep myself in check.

"And when I would wake up after dreaming of you, I would be so hard that I couldn't stop myself."

"Yes." I didn't need to tell him that I'd done the same, imagining the times we'd been together while slipping my hand between my legs and desperately wishing that he were close. There with me. Taking me the way that I wanted him to.

Slowly, Ethan added a second finger to the first, pushing in and out. I shuddered on his hand, surrendering to the feeling of him, loving it.

I wanted this. All of it.

Ethan's free hand settled behind my neck, guiding my face

135

closer in a silent command to look at him, and not look away. As if I wanted to look anywhere else.

He worked me with his fingers, faster, harder, curling them up and back to find the spot that made white light flash behind my eyes. "Ethan." His name left me on a groan, and my eyes fluttered closed.

Immediately, his fingers tightened on my neck. "Look at me." But he didn't stop moving. Stroking. Pushing heat and pleasure up into me with his fingers while I struggled to meet his gaze.

The minute I did, I was undone. I couldn't look at Ethan and hide. He knew me inside and out, just like I knew him. I didn't look away. His green eyes were my anchor in the dimness as I let go.

All the fear and the uncertainty of the past few days. The things that I hadn't let myself think about. The nerves I'd had over our relationship. All of that slipped away as I looked at him. Pleasure raced up my spine as I did, exploding outward and rendering me blind.

I squeezed against him, rocking my hips to beg for more. But I didn't move my hands from his shoulders. I held on for dear life, riding out that orgasm until it left me sagging, my head falling against his.

He let me catch my breath for a moment before he slipped out of me, and I moaned at the loss.

"You're so fucking beautiful, Jess. I've missed you so much."

I leaned forward and kissed him, daring to slip my hands behind his neck and yank him closer. His tongue stroked into my mouth the same way his fingers had stroked into me, and I wanted more.

"Now," he said.

I didn't need to ask him what he meant. We'd always been in sync enough to communicate without words, and I felt that coming back. I reached between us, fumbling with the cold metal of his belt for a moment before I could release him.

Ethan was so hot and so, so hard in my hands. I stroked along his length, and he hissed through his teeth. He was just as sensitive as I was—that made me smile.

His hands fell hard on my hips, lifting me so I was perched where he wanted. It seemed like it was nothing for him to hold me in the air and lower me slowly onto him. He might be quiet, but he was damned strong.

"Hands on my shoulders." He lowered me down. I just managed to do as he told me as he entered me, the feeling of him finally inside me overwhelming. Our bodies melded together inch by agonizing inch. It had been so long. He felt so good. By the time we settled together—Ethan buried to the hilt inside me—I was stretched full of him and could barely breathe.

I never wanted it to end.

Ethan was the only man I'd been with. Ever. And feeling him inside me now, I was so glad. Being with anyone else like this was . . . unthinkable. I couldn't imagine being this close— this intimate—with another person. I didn't care that I hadn't tried other men. Wouldn't ever want to.

I knew what I wanted, and that was Ethan. Always.

Breathless, I waited until I had adjusted to his size once again. Then I moved, rocking my hips. God he felt good. Deep, shuddering pleasure echoed through me as I rocked into him.

Until he stopped me. "No."

That was when he took full control. With his hands on my hips, he set the pace, thrusting up at the same time as he yanked me down onto him. Over, and over, and over. My body was already primed for pleasure, and every time he drove upward set off a new wave of perfect, glorious ecstasy.

His fingers dug into my hips, holding me still while he fucked me, somehow holding me on the edge of bliss without pushing me over. Faster and slower, he controlled the rhythm, taking exactly what he wanted.

"Please," I begged him.

"Please what?"

"More. You. More." Only Ethan could turn me into a mindless mess.

He gave it to me, driving into me with a force that stole all the air in my lungs. Every move he made plunged deep, finding that elusive spot deep inside me that made me see fireworks. A second orgasm rose like a wave and crashed over me. I was drowning in sensation. Drowning in him.

He captured my mouth with his, covering the cry that flew out of me. Like he knew exactly what I was going to do before I even did it.

Because he did. Ethan had always known me better than I knew myself.

With one last thrust, he called out my name, wrapping his arms around me and burying his face in my neck.

We held each other close in silence for long minutes.

"I know you said we need to talk about our future, but I don't want to talk about it," I finally said to him, still shuddering in the aftermath. "Not ever."

Ethan's voice was low. Rough. "Why?"

"Because there's not a question. It's you. It's always been you. It's only ever been you."

He searched my eyes in that earnest way that he had, and I could feel him inside me, still hard despite our lovemaking. "I don't want you to have regrets, Jess. If you want the freedom to explore, take it. I don't own you."

Using my body, I squeezed him. He did own me in every way that mattered. I was *his*.

"Jess," he said, almost in warning.

"I love that you would give me that freedom if it was what I needed," I said. "It's not. There's nobody I could

ever want more than you. Nobody I could have this with."
I squeezed him again. "I don't need intimacy with
someone else to let me know I only want intimacy with
you."

He rolled his hips into mine, making me gasp. No words.
His only response was to make me feel again. With sudden
movement, Ethan shifted us so we were once again on the
floor. He stretched over me, never once pulling away. And he
unleashed himself.

Before he'd said he'd wanted long and slow. This was
anything but. This was powerful and all-consuming. Frenzied
and desperate and damned hot. Most of all, he was illustrating
exactly how thoroughly he owned me. Even if he didn't think
he did.

Ethan grabbed my hands and laced our fingers together,
bracing them against the floor as he moved. I loved him like
this. It was like he was suddenly completely himself. With no
walls. Showing me the absolutely badass man that he was.

This time we were together. Our breath synced and bodies
moved as one. I sank into him, letting go of everything but this
moment and the shivering, shimmering pleasure sparkling
through me. Now I couldn't keep quiet, but my cries were lost
in the sound of the moving train.

His lips were on my neck, dragging across my skin as we
both crashed over the edge together. He jerked inside me and
filled me with that delicious heat I couldn't ignore.

He groaned my name, dragging it out. It was the sexiest
sound in the world.

There was no more darkness behind my eyes. Everything I
saw was light and perfect as I arched into one last brutal
climax. Sparks flew down my nerves. It lasted forever, and was
over far too soon, leaving us gasping for breath in each other's
arms.

Ethan looked down at me. "I love you." There was no

doubting the sincerity in his words. "More than you can ever know, Jess. You're it for me."

Tears blurred my vision once more, and I pulled him into a kiss. "You're it for me too. My Ethan."

Eventually, we moved, rearranging ourselves so we were clothed before Ethan pulled me back to him. He curled around me, my back against his chest. And we didn't need more words to understand what we meant to each other. No matter the space we'd let grow between us.

There was no place that I felt safer or happier than when Ethan was holding me.

We drifted for a while, and I think I fell asleep. It was the shrieking of the train's brakes and the jolting of the car that made me surge into awareness. I crawled away from Ethan, peering through the cracks in the slats of the car.

There was nothing outside but trees and countryside. Nothing to make me think we were close to an actual station. I looked back at Ethan and shook my head. We couldn't speak now.

This wasn't a scheduled stop, and that meant it could be a search of the train. We were no longer safe here. It was time to go.

CHAPTER EIGHTEEN

FIFTEEN YEARS AGO
   Ethan - 9
   Jess - 6

"Ethan?"

He shouldn't have come here. He knew Jess could see the hay bales from her bedroom window especially with a full moon like tonight. He hadn't meant to worry her or wake her up, but he hadn't known where else to go.

"Hey, Jess."

"Did you walk over here?"

"Yeah. Through the woods." It wasn't that far. Plus, he'd needed some time to think.

"Is everything okay?"

Jess was young. It was hard to remember how young she was when she was already doing school work way past Ethan's level. She was smart, but she was still young, and he didn't want to scare her.

But he was scared.

Jess lay down next to him on top of the pile of hay and slipped her hand into his. He immediately felt a little better.

"Is it about Aunt Wavy?" Jess asked.

He nodded, not surprised she'd already heard. It wasn't every day one of the town's favorite people was kidnapped by a terrorist group. A bad one.

"My dad cried." Ethan could barely get the words out himself. He'd never seen his dad cry.

The entire Linear Tactical team had been at his house, discussing plans and options. Ethan was supposed to have been in bed, but he'd snuck into the stairwell so he could hear.

But hearing his dad cry had scared him.

"They're going to find her," Jess whispered. "Mr. Ian really likes Aunt Wavy, and he has the whole Zodiac Tactical company. He'll get her back, and your dad will help."

"Do you really think so?"

She squeezed his hand. "I know so. They will get Aunt Wavy back. They love her too much not to."

Jess said it with such finality that Ethan's panic eased a bit. Dad had been in the Special Forces and Mr. Ian had been a Navy SEAL. They'd been trained to help people in dangerous situations. To rescue people.

"You're right. They will get her back because they're heroes."

"Yes." Jess brought her other hand around to hold his in both of hers. "That's right."

"Someday, I'm going to be a hero too. Just like them."

"I know." She said that with just as much finality too.

And Ethan believed.

CHAPTER NINETEEN

Jess

ETHAN JUMPED FIRST as the train slowed, and I followed. Landing on the ground jostled my bones, but I didn't have a choice. We couldn't afford to wait until the train stopped.

The sun was rising. We couldn't see the front of the train to get an idea of what was happening, but we definitely weren't going to stick around to see. Ethan took my hand and we slipped into the trees. Shouts came from the front of the train as we made it deeper into the woods. Luck was on our side. For the moment.

We quietly consulted the map, following the tracks on it until we could get an idea of where we were. It had cut more than half the distance off our journey, but we were still far away from the capital.

Ethan pointed in the direction that we needed to go. Neither of us wanted to speak, knowing that we were so close to possible enemies.

Passing through the woods, we found a dirt road heading in

the direction we needed. "I think it's safe enough to use it," Ethan said softly. "And it will be faster than moving through wilderness."

I nodded.

We walked hand in hand. Our intimacy of last night had carried over. We were a solid unit again, the way we'd always been as kids. The way I wanted us to always be.

But as happy as I was, I was tired. The couple hours of sleep that we'd managed to get was only a Band-Aid on the exhaustion that seeped through my pores. If—*when*—we got out of here, the first thing I wanted was a shower. Followed by a long nap. Preferably curled up next to Ethan. I always slept better when he was near.

The sound of tires in front of us came too quickly for us to hide, and the car turned around the corner into view in the next second. Ethan's hand tightened on mine. "Just keep walking," he said. "We're not doing anything wrong. Just out for a walk."

"In the middle of nowhere," I muttered.

"Pretend it's normal."

The car slowed down as it came toward us, and Ethan gave a friendly wave. The couple in the car stared at us for a moment as their car came to a stop. "Should we stop?" I asked Ethan as we kept walking toward them.

"No. Don't stop."

The woman in the car pointed at us and started speaking to the man. But speaking was an understatement. She was absolutely freaking out. The man nodded, agreeing. Neither of them took their eyes off us, and we walked casually past, their voices muffled as they argued.

As soon as we had passed the car, they took off, gravel spitting behind their tires. If this road had been asphalt, they would have burned rubber for sure.

"Fuck," Ethan said, low and urgent. "That's not good."

My stomach sank. "Does that mean what I think it means?"

He nodded, pulling me faster along the road. "They knew our faces. And they were civilians. So Radu has been circulating our pictures and has asked the general populace to help find us. Maybe offered a reward."

"How does he have that much influence?"

"Doesn't really matter," Ethan said. "He does. And that's going to make this much, much harder."

He pulled me off the road, and we ducked into the trees, going as fast as we dared. When we were out of hearing distance from the road, Ethan finally stopped. "I need to talk to Uncle Ian."

He pulled out the cellphone he had on him. "Is there a signal?"

"Not much, but enough." He quickly dialed a number and held the phone to his ear. I wrapped my arms around him and pressed my ear near to the phone so I could hear too. Ethan's free arm held me close, and I breathed in the scent of him while the phone rang.

Ian's voice was quiet, but I could hear him well enough. "Ethan?"

"Yeah."

"Thank God. I heard from Landon and Isaac, and they brought me up to speed, but they said they hadn't heard from you."

Ethan sighed. "We're okay. We hopped a train trying to get to Kishinev but had to get off. On foot is just as bad. Radu has circulated our photos. We just passed two civilians who knew us, which means that Radu will have our location soon. I don't know if we're going to make it to Kishinev in time for the extract. Not if we have to stay out of sight the whole time."

Ian let out a string of curses I'm not sure he would have used if he'd known I was listening. "This situation is actually worse than that. 'Radu' is Andre Radu."

"Shit." Ethan hung his head. "Are you serious?"

"Who is Radu, Uncle Ian?" I asked.

"Jess, I'm glad you're okay, honey," Ian said. "Andre Radu is a weapons and information dealer. One of the terrorist world's top resources. He doesn't commit the crimes, but he makes sure the actual terrorists have everything that they need. This is not a good guy."

I looked up into Ethan's eyes. They were grim.

"I know you both already know this, but Radu cannot get his hands on the stolen research. Isaac and Landon filled me in on the details about Alena but said she doesn't have it."

"Affirmative," Ethan said. "It's safe with us."

"Then I'll feel a hell of a lot better when you're out of the country. If Radu has circulated your photos, getting into the city will be impossible. But we have a backup."

"Where?" Ethan handed me the phone and dug in the backpack for the map. He spread it on the ground and I held up the phone so we could both hear.

"An airstrip west of the city. It's only used for commercial shipments, so it's farther out. Should be a little closer to you and isolated enough that you can get there."

Ethan found the spot. "Got it."

"Where is that relative to where you are?"

"We can be there in roughly three hours," Ethan said, looking at me. "If we push."

I nodded. I would do whatever we needed to do to get out of here. And if that meant pushing myself past my limits for a few hours, then so be it.

"My pilot will meet you there," Ian said. "In three and fifteen, to give you a little wiggle room. But this pickup isn't going to be pretty."

Ethan chuckled. "It never is."

"Quick and dirty. I don't want the plane to be on the

ground for more than thirty seconds. So when you get there, be ready to run and board."

"We can do that," I said.

"Good," he said, though he didn't sound relieved at all. "Also, very important. You need to know—"

The phone went dead, and a beep told me that the connection had failed.

"Shit." Ethan took the phone from me and redialed, but I watched the call fail while it was still on the screen.

"What happened?"

He shook his head. "There's suddenly no signal at all. Not even a blip. It's just a flat line."

Adrenaline spiked through me. "Think it's artificial?"

"Yeah," he said, dropping his voice further. "If Radu and his men are using signal blockers, at least some of them have to be close. We have to be as quiet as possible, but we also have to be fast."

Not to mention we had no idea what really important thing Ian had to tell us.

I nodded. "I'll keep up."

For a brief second, Ethan hauled me against him and captured my lips with his. The kiss was filled with heat and a promise—that he would do whatever he could to get us out.

Then he pulled away, and we were moving. We had a plane to catch.

The terrain here wasn't so different than what I'd grown up hiking in Wyoming. There were fewer mountains here, but that made it easier for us.

Whenever we broke out of the trees, and there was nothing but an open field in front of us, we ran. There wasn't any point in moving slowly through an open field that made us easy targets.

Despite my familiarity with the terrain, Ethan was so much better at this than I was. He never seemed to tire, and the rocks and hills that we had to climb looked effortless for him to scale. Obviously, his SEAL training had only furthered what he'd spent a lifetime doing in Wyoming.

But I held my own. I wasn't as graceful, and I lagged behind a little. But Ethan didn't have to slow his pace too much for me, and I was proud of that.

Judging by the looks Ethan kept giving me, he was proud of me too. He led the way, and I followed. He helped me climb things that were just out of my reach, and I helped him with the map the few times we stopped to get our bearings. As always, we made a good team.

I wanted to revel in the fact that he was proud of me. I wanted to lie down and go to sleep. I wanted so many things that didn't matter in this moment because our lives depended on me not stopping. So I didn't stop.

We skirted a wooded area. Over the past couple of hours, we hadn't seen any people, but the way Ethan was moving now —slowly and cautiously—made me think his instincts felt something that I did not.

Moving through the trees, we both did our best to go as silently as possible, though that slowed our pace to a crawl.

To our left, a branch snapped. Both of us froze in place. My heart thundered in my ears and everything around us seemed suddenly loud. The wind. The rustle of branches. Birdsong.

Ethan held out a hand to me, telling me to stay put. He ventured forward alone, looking around, and I held my breath. It felt like the woods themselves were suddenly thick with tension.

He was so fast, I could barely see him. Like a snake striking, Ethan leapt out from behind the tree where he was hiding and raised his tranq gun in the same motion, firing. Instantly, he dropped to his knees and spun and fired again, before the first body hit the ground.

I heard two dull thuds as the men fell, but I didn't move

until Ethan did. He looked them over, taking a large gun from one of the men and tossing it away. But he took one of the pistols and kept it.

I just stared at him. Awed. It was one thing to know that he'd made a career out of being an utter badass. It was an entirely different thing to see him in action.

"That's it," he said. "I'm out of tranquilizers."

I swallowed. "Hopefully, we won't need them."

"Hopefully not."

"These were Radu's men?"

Ethan shrugged. "Even if they weren't, they were heavily armed. Not something to take a chance with. But I'm going to go with yes." We stood still for another moment, just resting. And then Ethan looked at me. "Ready?"

"Ready," I said, as if we had any other options. Time was ticking, and we still had a ways to go. So we moved, not bothering as much with stealth as we were with speed.

Maybe it was the adrenaline that had pumped through my system at the near miss with the men in the woods, but after that I couldn't seem to get my energy back up. I was starting to drag. My body ached from running and climbing. My feet screamed that they had had enough, and my stomach had numbed the feeling of hunger hours ago. I kept going, but it was getting harder.

Ethan's hand found mine and didn't let go. The message was clear: he wasn't leaving me. My pace would be his pace.

I never felt more relief than when I saw the airfield in front of us. We'd made it. It was almost over. All we had to do was wait for the plane, then one more sprint. I could do that much.

Breaking out of the final line of trees, we stumbled to a stop and Ethan pulled me into a hug. "You did amazing," he whispered in my ear. "You are amazing."

Tears stung my eyes, and I buried my face in his chest. I

wasn't a big crier, but I couldn't stop them right now. We were so close, and I wanted it to be over.

The screech of tires made me jump. A jeep careened toward us from the far end of the runway, moving toward us too fast to not know what they were looking for.

They knew we were here.

"Go." Ethan pulled me back toward the trees where we'd just come from.

We didn't make it far. I skidded to a stop barely inside the tree line when half a dozen men met us there coming from the other direction. They were obviously here to take us.

Ethan was already moving, taking one down with a quick punch to the face. I followed his lead. One of the guys grabbed me from behind, and I didn't hesitate—I threw my head back with as much force as I could. The guy howled as his nose broke, and I jumped away, ready to fight another.

I managed to land a hit on another one, hoping—*knowing*—Ethan could hold his own. I would fight by his side, not be a damsel that he had to protect.

But the click of a hammer and a barrel against my skull made me freeze. One of them wrapped an arm across my chest, the pistol pushed into my head hard enough to bruise.

And in front of me, Ethan was a whirlwind. Three men were on the ground, and he was fighting a fourth when I called his name. "Ethan."

He froze when he saw me, hands instantly in the air. The soldier he was fighting hit him in the stomach. He took it well, though it knocked the wind out of his lungs. But he never looked away from me. Our eyes were locked.

We'd been so close. What would happen when Ian's pilot got here? Would they try to land anyway? Would they leave us completely? I didn't know.

The jeep we saw at a distance stopped in front of us, and Radu's men marched us both closer to the tarmac. I felt sick.

Radu himself got out of the driver's seat, a smug smile on his face. But I expected that from him now that I knew who he was.

But even worse was who got out beside him, with a smile just as smug.

Alena.

CHAPTER TWENTY

Jess

ALENA SMIRKED at me as she jumped down from the Jeep. "See? I knew this is where they would come."

"So you did," Radu said. He seemed more than a little annoyed, but his eyes were still steady on Ethan and me.

The look on Alena's face was victorious. Deep down, I hadn't wanted to believe that it was real. I'd hoped there had been some sort of mistake. But the woman in front of me was not the woman I had become friends with over the past two years.

This person was hard. She had anger and cruelty in her gaze. As she took in my predicament, gun pressed to my temple, she broke into a full smile.

"Looks like you're not the only genius around. It was almost pathetically easy to avoid your attempts to find the mole. It was simple to plant suggestions that you took without question. And now look at you. Even that famous brain isn't enough to save you from a bullet, Dr. O'Conner."

She was right. My PhD in biotechnology wasn't going to save me.

"Why are you doing this?" The soldier holding me pressed the gun harder into my skull, and I winced. "I don't believe this is who you are."

"You don't know shit about me or who I am."

I shook my head before remembering the gun and going still. "How can you say that?"

"The most prestigious biotechnology program in the world and all the main recipients are independently wealthy. Do you know how absolutely fucked that is? Your father is a musician that the whole world knows. Russell's father is a billionaire. An actual, literal billionaire. And Susan's family has money too."

"So you're going to sell off our research?"

"You don't know what it's like to scrape for everything you have. You've never been poor. You've never had to work for anything in your life. It's all been handed to you because of your pretty blue eyes and the fact that you're smart. But I've worked for *everything*. And finally it's paying off. I'll never be poor again after this."

I swallowed. "Alena. Please. You can't do this. You know who Radu is? What he'll do with the research? He assists terrorists. He'll make sure our information gets into the hands of people who will use it for the most harm."

Alena knew exactly what our research was and how it could be twisted. A sickening realization hit me. Alena was the one who'd pushed us in that direction. We'd discussed as a team the possibility of weaponization. She'd been the one to argue that we should continue along that line anyway.

She'd planned this from the beginning.

"You did it on purpose," I said. "You pushed us to research what we did so that you could sell it. That's all you ever wanted. How deep does this go, Alena? Did you join the fellowship program knowing that you would do this?"

"Yes," she said simply. "To all of it. Yes, I know exactly who he is, and I don't care. We're both useful to each other. Radu can give me what I've always deserved, and in the process teach a lesson to all you rich people who insist on looking down on the rest of us."

I couldn't stop the small cry that escaped me at her words. Ethan's gaze snapped to mine, checking to see if I was all right. I wasn't. I was the furthest thing from all right.

Everything I'd said on the train last night was true. This was my fault, and I should have seen it. Now we were in this mess, and I honestly didn't know if we would make it out alive.

"I never meant to make you feel like I looked down on you, Alena. I'm so sorry. I grew up for a long time without money too. My mother cleaned houses for a living until my father came into our lives."

Alena's face went utterly cold. "So smart, aren't you? Trying to emotionally manipulate me. Make it seem like we're alike. We're *nothing* alike. Although I'll soon be rich. But you'll be too dead to appreciate the new similarity."

This was bad. I didn't know how much of Alena's true personality was a lie, but there was one thing I knew about her. Once she decided on something, she was done. That was the decision. She'd already thought through all the options and all the ramifications. And she'd decided what she wanted to do to me a long time ago.

There was no way that Ian's pilot could land. There was enough firepower here that they would simply shoot down the plane if he tried. There was no getting out of this.

I looked at Ethan, panic crawling up my throat. This couldn't be the end of everything. We couldn't have worked so hard to make our way back to each other only to die. I would not accept that. Could not.

"It doesn't have to be this way, Alena." I had to think. Figure out a plan. A weakness.

She opened her mouth to go at me again, but Radu cut her off. "Enough. Your drama makes no one any money."

He walked toward me slowly, and the way he was looking at me made my skin crawl. The first time I'd seen him, he hadn't known which of us actually had the research. He'd only known that it wasn't Alena.

Now that he knew, he looked at me like a starving dog looked at a raw steak: absolute, feral desire. To him, now, I represented millions of dollars. Maybe hundreds of millions. I wasn't a person in his eyes, and he wasn't going to treat me like one.

Radu stopped in front of me, barely a foot away, and looked me up and down. He nodded to the soldier holding me, and the man let me go. I stumbled but managed to stay upright. His gun was no longer against my head. I didn't have to look over my shoulder to know it was pointed at me from behind.

Radu took a cigarette out and lit it. Everything about his stance was casual, as if it were completely normal to have guns trained on people. In his life, it probably was.

When he spoke, the words were quiet. "I know a lot about you, Jess O'Conner. Alena has told me that you're the shining star of the program. The mind that a thousand people would kill for, and much of the reason the research you stole is so valuable to me." Another drag on his cigarette. "I appreciate that. And I want to give credit where it's due. So thank you for your contribution."

I said nothing. I didn't want his praise. If I'd known that what we were studying had anything to do with him, I would have stopped it. I would have tried to lead us down a different path.

"Now that I've done that," he said, "I need you to give me the research."

My throat was dry, the lie scraping past. "I don't have it."

Pain exploded through the side of my face as Radu's fist

crashed into it. Ethan shouted, and a scuffle broke out. It was so sudden and blinding that I didn't know how I'd gotten to the ground.

When I blinked the pain from my eyes, Ethan was now on his knees, two soldiers forcibly holding his arms behind him. His body was straining, and I had no doubt that if he managed to get free, he would kill Radu with his bare hands.

A word spoken in Moldovan, and I was hauled to my feet again, dizzy, head throbbing. The hands on me forced me to face Radu. He was still calm, like he didn't have a care in the world.

"You might think I'm a killer," he said. "But I don't like to kill unnecessarily."

He pulled out a gun and made a motion I'd seen a thousand times in my life: the smooth slide of the barrel as he chambered a round.

Growing up with people who taught survival skills, I'd quickly learned to spot when someone was familiar with weapons. Radu breathed them. The gun was an extension of his body, and this man wouldn't give me a second thought after he put a bullet through my head. I could see it in his eyes.

He may not like to kill unnecessarily, but what he did not say was that my death was necessary if I didn't give him what I wanted.

My heart pounded, and I tried to calm myself down.

When I was younger, I'd wondered what I would do if I were in a situation like this—like the ones the Linear Tactical guys told me about. I liked to think that I would be brave and walk into the arms of death without flinching.

But right now, I didn't want to. I was terrified and didn't want to die. I wanted to have the life I'd grown up picturing with Ethan. Our family. But it was disappearing right in front of me. All the color drained from the world.

Radu pointed the gun at my forehead. "The research," he says. "I won't ask you again."

I took a breath, gathering every ounce of my courage, and looked Radu straight in the eye. If there was one thing that I'd learned in my life, it was to look my enemies in the eye without flinching.

If he killed me, they would never find the chip. Ethan would never give it up. "I told you I don't have it."

Radu pulled down the hammer, and I closed my eyes.

"Allow me to handle her," Alena said, stepping up beside Radu.

I caught the surprise on his face when I opened my eyes again. But he handed her the gun. What was most likely here? What would Alena do? Would she shoot me in the knee and try to torture me into talking? At this point I wouldn't put it past her.

But it was so much worse. Alena walked the short distance to where Ethan was still kneeling and pressed the gun to his head. All the air in my lungs disappeared. The world slowed down.

Of course she would do this. She knew how I felt about Ethan. I'd told her everything about him. How deeply I loved him. How we'd been together our whole lives. How he knew me better than I knew myself.

She knew that out of anything in the world, Ethan was my greatest weakness. I would do anything I could to save him.

And this time I couldn't.

Ethan looked at me and gave me the slightest nod. He knew. I blinked back sudden tears because this was the worst thing I could imagine. What was on the tiny chip around my neck was worth more than his life. And my life.

We had to protect it, even if that meant that I was about to watch him die, and I would die a moment afterward.

He nodded again, telling me that he understood and that

he was ready. Love shone from his green eyes in a way I'd never seen. A way that said he'd loved me with all his being in this life, and he would find me in the next and love me just as hard.

I couldn't stop the sob that escaped me.

And then Ethan, my silent Ethan, began to speak. "Did I tell you why I got out of the Navy, Jess? I got out because after I came to London, I realized that I couldn't live without you anymore. I was done spending years apart from you. I love you. More than anything. More than life itself. Our entire lives, I've loved only you." The rest of the words were unspoken. He would continue to love me after the end of our lives. Even if that was right now.

Tears spilled over, my breath ragged. I couldn't look away from him.

But now his eyes were different. Still full of love, always full of love, but more determined. Strategic.

He tilted his head to the right, down toward the ground. It looked uncomfortable. Not a natural motion. He caught my eyes and then looked at the ground. And then he did it again.

"I bought a ring," he said. "And my plan was to ask you for forever as soon as we got home. Because you are my forever, Jess."

The words struck me in the heart, but he was still looking at me and then the ground, nearly frantic, though his expression was neutral. Ethan knew something I didn't, and he was trying to let me know. The ground. The only thing I could think of was to fall.

"We'll build a house," he said, continuing to talk and slumping his shoulders like he might keel over. He looked at the ground again. "Anywhere you want. We can do it ourselves."

"Quiet," Radu said, and turned to me. "Enough. You choose. Your man with all his love words or the chip. Right now."

My eyes were still on Ethan. I didn't dare look away. His mouth rounded in a single word.

Now.

I dropped to the ground, letting all my weight collapse. The guards holding me didn't expect it, and their hands slipped off me. Then everything happened at once. The distinct sound of silenced gunshots rang out, audible in every direction like an echo.

Everybody around me fell to the ground, as if someone had switched off the power button. Radu, Alena, and all the soldiers dropped like lifeless dolls.

That was all I saw before a body landed on mine, hard. Ethan.

He covered me, not caring at all if he caught one of the flying bullets. His hands wrapped around my head. If something deadly was going to get to me, it was going to have to go through him first.

I pushed at him, unable to stop the words that spilled out of me, even though at this moment they should be the last thing on my mind. "You bought me a *ring?*"

His head lifted so we were eye to eye. "I did," he whispered. "I love you, Jess. So fucking much. You're my everything."

His lips were hot on mine, our bodies so close as he kept protecting me.

Around us I heard the sounds of struggle, and then nothing. The quiet that followed was louder than everything else had been.

An amused chuckle. "You can get off her now."

I shook my head, blinking. That voice could not possibly be right. "*Daddy?*"

Ethan slipped off me and helped me stand. It was my dad. And not just him, but Ethan's dad, Uncle Finn, and most of the other Linear Tactical team. Zac Mackay. Gavin Zimmerman. Dorian Lindstrom and his wife, Ray.

"What?" I asked. "How?"

Ethan hugged his dad while I hugged mine.

"As soon as Ian told us what was going on, I got the team together and got them over here myself in case unofficial backup was needed," Dad said. "One of the perks of being famous is that the government allowed me and my posse in to visit as long as I promised to do a show."

"Ian was supposed to let you know we were headed your way from town," Finn said. "But he lost contact with you."

Ethan still had his arm around his dad. "When I heard the plane, I knew it was too big for what Uncle Ian would've sent just for us. But believe me, I've never been happier than to see you signaling me from the woods."

"You guys handled yourself well," Zac said. "If you hadn't been able to communicate to little Jess that she needed to drop, taking them out would've been a lot more difficult."

Little Jess. They'd called me that for most of my life, even as an adult. But today they got a free pass.

"Are Landon and Isaac okay?" Ethan asked. "Alena had intel on where they were going."

Finn nodded. "Yes, they've already gotten Russell and Susan to safety."

Gavin looked around. "We need to head out before any government officials arrive. Let's get Ian on the phone and see how he wants to handle the mess we've made here."

Dorian grinned. "Plus, I hear there's an impromptu Cade Conner show in town tonight. We don't want to miss that."

Dad looked at Ethan. "And you and I need to have a chat, I think. One time about fifteen years ago, you sat me down to have a man-to-man about Jess and what she deserved. Now I think it's my turn to return the favor."

CHAPTER TWENTY-ONE

Ethan

"Got any doubts, son?"

Dad and I sat in the small vestibule behind the altar of the church. It was almost time for me to go out, for me to watch as Jess walked down the aisle and became my bride.

I grinned. Dad would be standing beside me as my best man, just the way I'd wanted it. My teenage brothers were serving as ushers, and my *oops-surprise!* three-year-old baby sister was a flower girl.

"Not a single one since I was seven years old and a little tornado blew into my life."

Dad chuckled. "She is a force of nature, isn't she?"

"Just like Mom." And Dad still looked at Charlie like the sun and the moon hung on her. He'd done that for as long as I could remember. And he'd probably continue doing it until the day he died.

It was almost time for us to go out; most of the guests had

been seated in the small church. I glanced out the door's tinted window to get a look at our friends and family filling the pews.

"Why does Uncle Gabe look like he might kill Boy Riley?"

Dad broke out into a huge grin. "Evidently, Boy Riley's twins talked Gabe's twins into sneaking out last weekend. Tucker and Colton are smitten with Gabe's girls, and they have no fear, just like their dad."

I chuckled. "In my mind, all those kids are five years old." That's how old both sets of twins had been when I'd left Oak Creek, close to my brother Derek's age.

"But in reality, those kids are twelve and thirteen now. Just starting to get into trouble. Seeing Gabe lose his shit over his two daughters, since they have Jordan's looks, makes my day on a regular occasion."

I wondered if I should remind Dad that he had a daughter now too, and she had *Charlie's* looks. He'd be losing his shit soon enough.

"And I see Lincoln is sitting back by himself, not with the other kids."

Dad shrugged. "You know Lincoln."

My thirteen-year-old cousin didn't really get along with kids his own age. He'd been special since the time he was born—actually before he was born. Early tests had suggested to Uncle Baby and Aunt Quinn that Lincoln was likely to have Down syndrome.

He hadn't. The opposite, in fact.

Lincoln was brilliant in the same way Jess was brilliant, except where Jess was also great with people and tended to be a social butterfly, Lincoln would much prefer to keep to himself.

"Has he decided whether to take the Vandercroft fellowship?"

Dad shook his head. "I don't think so. Not yet. Lincoln isn't like Jess. Baby and Quinn don't feel like they can just send him to a school somewhere being so young."

I nodded. "Jess could handle it, but she was unique, for sure. Going to a foreign country at fourteen isn't for everyone, no matter how smart they are."

"And besides, I think Lincoln got a hold of Neo and Kendrick's computers and they taught him some stuff."

I rolled my eyes. "Hacking stuff?"

Dad fought back a smile. "Is there anything else with those two? Anyway, Lincoln really liked it."

Great. The kid had an off-the-charts IQ, but he was also almost painfully introverted. He needed guidance or he could easily slip in the wrong direction.

Dad walked over and slapped me on the shoulder at the door. "Don't worry about Lincoln. We're all keeping an eye on him. We're not going to let him wander too far. It's just a matter of helping him find his path."

That was true. With an extended family like this, Lincoln wasn't going to wander too far.

"Why don't you quit worrying about everyone else," Dad said, "and let's get you out there and married."

I nodded; it was time. It was beyond time.

We'd been back from Moldova exactly one month—after stopping in London to return the research and meet with the research heads there, and then Washington, DC for a debriefing.

Jess and I hadn't wanted to wait any longer to get married. A gun at the temple of the person who meant the most to you in the world taught you very quickly not to put off your forever.

The organ started playing, and Dad and I took our place at the front of the church. I turned and watched as my younger brother Thomas walked Peyton, Jess's mom, down the aisle and escorted her into her seat.

Then my youngest brother, Derek, walked Mom down the

aisle, seating her in the opposite row. She caught my eye and stuck her tongue out at me.

This woman may not have given birth to me, but she was my mother in every other way. She'd saved my life more than once, and I loved her to distraction.

Next, Jess's sister, Ella, walked down the aisle. She was the maid of honor. If things had not gone so horribly wrong, it would have been Alena here as the maid of honor. But Jess and I had agreed that having Ella stand beside Jess was just as special.

We'd decided to keep the wedding small, mostly because of the last-minute nature, but also because the people most important to us were the ones in this town. My SEAL team had promised they would celebrate my new nuptials at a later date. They were off on a mission, and I understood. I was on my own mission.

My sister, River, was next as the flower girl. She preened in her pretty dress and took out one flower petal at a time from her basket and placed it on the ground as she walked. Nobody dared correct her. River did things however she wanted to do them, and that was okay with everyone else. By the time she was finished, there was a straight line of petals and a church full of grinning people.

And then Jess was there, standing at the door of the church on her father's arm. The wedding march began, and she moved confidently toward me. Jess did everything with confidence. It was one of the things I loved most about her.

My smile grew bigger with every step she took. There was no other place in the entire world I'd rather be right now than standing here waiting for her.

She reached the front and Cade pulled the veil back from her face and kissed her on the cheek. He winked at me and then placed her hand in mine without hesitation. That trust was not something I took lightly.

We turned and the preacher said words. I'm sure I was supposed to be listening to them, but I couldn't. All I could do was feel Jess beside me, breathe in her scent. And know I was the luckiest man on the planet because I hadn't had to look around to find what I wanted. She had been there with me the whole time.

I'd never had to kiss another woman. Never wanted to kiss another woman. *Would* never want to kiss another woman.

Jess would hold all my kisses her whole life.

The preacher said other stuff. And we lit a candle, and Cade sang a song he'd written just for us. And then it was time for our vows.

Dad handed me the ring, and I rested it at the tip of her ring finger. My thumb stroked her palm as I looked into her blue eyes.

The vows I'd written weren't eloquent, but they were the truth.

"Jess, my heart married you the first day I met the little blonde four-year-old whose smile lit up my world. I'm glad the rest of me is catching up now. We have been each other's our whole life, and we will be each other's for the rest of our lives. I promise to love, honor, and protect you. Even when that means protecting you from yourself."

She smiled and slid her ring onto my finger. "You are *my Ethan*. I have known for as long as I can remember that you were mine and I was yours. You are the kindest, most generous, sexiest man I've ever known."

She broke into a grin as people snickered around us.

"No matter where my career goes, choosing you will be my greatest accomplishment in this lifetime. There is nothing I will ever be prouder of than being my Ethan's wife."

The preacher said some more words, but Jess and I just kept looking at each other and grinning. And finally he said the words we were both waiting to hear.

"I now pronounce you husband and wife. You may kiss your bride."

Jess threw her arms around my neck, and I wrapped mine around her waist and lifted her until she was off the ground.

And we kissed.

We'd had many firsts over the years, and we would have many more. But this was a special first, and I cherished it.

I let her go and set her back down on her feet. Ella handed her the bouquet, and we walked hand in hand down the aisle as husband and wife.

Ready for our forever.

CHAPTER TWENTY-TWO

Seventeen Years Ago
Ethan - 7
Jess - 4

Ethan sat on the front step of the Linear Tactical office. He had to stay out here until Dad was finished with his meeting.

He liked hanging out here during summer break, even though Dad had to work. There were toys in the back room of the office, and Ethan was allowed to run around outside wherever he wanted.

But he wished he had a friend. The kids at school made fun of him because he couldn't read, so he didn't like to hang out with them. It was easier to be by himself.

But he wished he had someone who could be just his.

A few seconds later, a little girl came running around the side of the building. She had long blonde hair and really big blue eyes. She smiled up at him.

"Hi! My name is Jess! My mom works here! Want to play with me?"

He smiled. She seemed really excited at the thought of them playing together. She was a girl, and younger, but he didn't care. She was friendly. He liked her.

He'd have to look out for her, probably. Make sure she stayed safe. But he didn't mind. He'd take care of her.

"Sure. I'm Ethan."

She nodded, touching a strand of that blonde hair with her fingers as she studied him. "My Ethan."

He shrugged. "Okay." Sounded good to him.

Then she grabbed his hand and pulled him off on an adventure.

*****

Thank you for reading FOREVER! The Linear Tactical characters you love are back in CODE NAME: ARIES.

ACKNOWLEDGMENTS

I knew from the first time Jess and Ethan showed up way back in EAGLE that they were going to have their own book. I didn't know how long the Linear Tactical series would end up being, but I knew Jess and Ethan's book, their FOREVER, would end it.

The thought of two people who knew they were meant for each other from the moment they met and never swaying from that knowledge was an absolute delight to write.

And, I'm a little biased, but I think this story was exactly what the series needed to wrap it all up.

(Side note: I never considered having a LINEAR TACTI-CAL: NEXT GENERATION series until writing Jess and Ethan's wedding scene. And now I'm like: *maybe these Oak Creek kids are going to have stories to tell too.*

No promises, but also, for the first time…not a definite *no*.)

A special thanks to my editors and proofers of FOREVER: Marci, Susan, Marilize, Tesh, and Dee. Plus, Elizabeth at Razor Sharp Editing. I appreciate your dedication and keen eyes. Thank you!

It's hard to move on from a beloved favorite, but I hope

you'll take the leap with me into my next series: Zodiac Tactical. I think you're going to love these books!

Sure, they're different, but the chemistry, the action, the community that becomes a family? Those elements are every bit as much a part of the Zodiac books as they were the Linear Tactical ones.

I can't wait to bring you Ian and Wavy's full story.

Most importantly, thank you, my reader friend, for taking this journey with me. It has been my honor and privilege to write the Linear Tactical books.

Believe in heroes,
    Janie

ABOUT THE AUTHOR

"Passion that leaps right off the page." - Romantic Times Book Reviews

USA Today and Publishers Weekly bestselling author Janie Crouch writes what she loves to read: passionate romantic suspense featuring protective heroes. Her books have won multiple awards, including the National Readers Choice and Booksellers' Best.

After a six-year stint in Germany (due to her husband's job as support for the U.S. Military) Janie is back on U.S. soil and loves hanging out with her four teenagers. Sometimes.

When she's not listening to the voices in her head—and even when she is—she enjoys engaging in all sorts of crazy adventures (200-mile relay races; Ironman Triathlons, treks to Mt. Everest Base Camp) traveling, and trying new recipes.

Her favorite quote: "Life is a daring adventure or nothing." ~ Helen Keller.

facebook.com/janiecrouch
amazon.com/author/janiecrouch
instagram.com/janiecrouch
bookbub.com/authors/janie-crouch

Printed in the USA
CPSIA information can be obtained
at www.ICGtesting.com
LVHW091251150224
771960LV00006B/179

9 781950 802326